Macabre Alley

by

I0536817

William Blackwell

Macabre Alley

Published by William Blackwell Publishing
Paperback ISBN: 978-1-0697318-8-3
Version: 2022.11.03

Don't let pain define you, let it refine you.
—Tim Fargo

I know without a doubt that our country and world will survive this pandemic. And just like our broken family, this broken world will be way more beautiful.
—Vicki Bunke

Hope is being able to see that there is light despite all of the darkness.
— Desmond Tutu

Contents

Fear Sells

"Fear sells," Andrew Robinson said. "Fear over nothing. It's all a bunch of fake shit politicians invented to rile the population."

The words hit Jamie McIntyre like a punch in the face. He had to bite his tongue to avoid smashing his friend in the face. They sat in Jamie's garage on the man-cave couch in suburban Calgary, Alberta, on a wintery Sunday afternoon swilling a few beers and trying—and evidently failing miserably—to solve all the world's problems.

Shit had splattered the fan when the subject of the global pandemic surfaced. And Jamie knew only too well the deadly seriousness of it.

COVID-19 is a highly infectious disease caused by a newly discovered coronavirus that originated in China. It produces mild flu-like symptoms in some, no symptoms in others, and dire symptoms and quick and horrible death in others. It had hit the world by storm early in 2020. It took everybody by surprise. About ten months later, over 80 million people worldwide infected. Over two million dead. Worldwide lockdowns. Hospitals overwhelmed. A new normal where social distancing, self-isolation, mask-wearing, and regular hand-sanitizing were practiced.

Most countries, including Canada, were ill-prepared to deal with the pandemic. Many politicians implemented Band-Aid measures, short lockdowns or no lockdowns, in an effort to balance political and economic interests with public health. In large part, these measures failed. In January, 2020, Theresa Tam, Canada's chief public health officer, said, "The risk of an outbreak in Canada remains low." Ten months later, Canada saw over 500,000 COVID-19 infections and over 18,000 deaths. A few months later, Canada was breaking records, averaging over 2,000 new cases per day. There was no comprehensive national pandemic management strategy to speak of. Prime Minister Justin Trudeau, for the most part, had left it up to the individual leaders of individual provinces to manage their fates. Some succeeded marginally; others failed dismally.

At that time, the United States had fared the worst in the world. Over 25 million infections. Over 400,000 deaths. Some states averaging a coronavirus death every six minutes and the US averaging over 1000 coronavirus deaths per day.

Unprecedented economic devastation crippled economies worldwide. Massive government bail-outs, huge deficits, and thousands of businesses went bankrupt.

How dare he? Jamie thought, understanding the full devastation caused by the pandemic.

This fool with his smug know-it-all attitude has the gall to call the pandemic 'a bunch of fake shit politicians invented to rile the population.'

Jamie drank the remainder of his beer in three gulps, tossed the can into a plastic garbage can, and reached into the cooler for another. He had a feeling he was gonna need as much liquid courage as he could pour down his throat for what was about to transpire.

"Why would governments want to rile the population?" Jamie asked.

Andrew burped loudly, tossed his empty in the garbage can, and reached for another. Popping it open, he ran a hand through his greasy blonde hair. "Fear sells, like I said. People get riled and scared, buy into it, and the government uses their fear to manipulate them. Control the population."

"Are you saying the pandemic is a hoax?"

"That's exactly what I'm saying. It's fake. If I knew someone who had tested positive, just to prove my point, I'd hug them, kiss them, and even lick their face. Just to prove it's all fake."

Jamie had known Andrew for over ten years and had never known his friend to be a conspiracy theorist. A digital marketing graduate, Andrew earned his living working on computers. But, Jamie supposed, it took something like a global pandemic to bring the fucking morons out of the woodwork. Not only that, since Andrew was on the computer for at least ten hours a day, he was certainly susceptible to all the misinformation and disinformation floating around about the pandemic. Conspiracy theories were rampant. The sad and dangerous fact was people had access to them with the click of a button. And they were believing them. And that was deadly-dangerous, especially when it led to disregarding and even flaunting public health measures designed to curtail the spread of the virus.

Jamie was close to exploding, but for the hell of it, he decided to give his friend—*not for long*—a little more rope to hang himself. He wanted to know exactly what hare-brained conspiracy theory Andrew was buying into.

"If it's a hoax, and the government created it, then why?" Jamie asked.

"Here's the deal," Andrew said. "Governments around the world have banded together—conspired—to create an elite population. The pandemic is a way for them to cull the masses.

They get people believing that the pandemic is real, then they develop a vaccine—as you know Canada has purchased millions of doses already—and inject the population with it, killing off all the idiots."

"I'll give you a little more rope. What else do you think?"

"If a person dies of a heart attack, drowning, even a car accident, doctors around the world call it a COVID death. If you have any lung issues at all, you would be considered to have the virus. If you end up in the hospital and get put on a ventilator, the ventilator will kill you. This whole mask-wearing measure is nothing more than fearmongering. A mask won't protect you from a virus. It will only protect you from a bacterial infection."

In spite of his best efforts to control his temper, Jamie detonated, picking up on one of Andrew's brain-dead points: "If the government is trying to cull the population—kill the idiots—they should start with *you*. That is the fucking stupidest shit I've heard all day."

Andrew slid clear to the other end of the couch, far away from Jamie. His eyes narrowed and his face whitened. "You'll fucking find out. Wait until we start vaccinating on a massive scale and you'll see tons of people dying."

"I can't believe someone as seemingly intelligent as you are is buying into this shit. And I suppose, even though we are in lockdown right now because of skyrocketing COVID cases, you're flaunting health measures. Probably not wearing a mask, not washing your hands, and sure as hell not social distancing."

"Why should I bother?" Andrew said. "It's all government-manufactured bullshit. Let me ask you this: Do you actually know anyone who has COVID?"

Jamie balled his fists and wracked his brain. He didn't have a large social circle. His mother, father, brother, and sister lived in Ontario and he had a handful of friends whom he saw occasionally. None of them had it as far as he knew. Wait. His job-site, a high-rise construction project in downtown Calgary, had recently been shut down because of a COVID outbreak. Two contractors had contracted the disease, although they worked five floors above Jamie and he didn't actually know them.

That wouldn't do.

Or maybe it would. He had to try to penetrate this fuck's thick skull. "My construction job was shut down recently due to an outbreak. I can't say I know the guys who tested positive but I know who they are. It's only a matter of time before someone we know either dies of the virus or gets really sick from it. And, before you try and sidetrack me, I have to warn you. Don't fucking flaunt the health measures. They were put in place to protect us and keep us safe."

"Like fuck they were."

"Your complete disregard for public health measures is scary. You could easily get infected, maybe have no symptoms, and walk around spreading it to everyone you come in contact with. Let's say you infect an elderly person or someone with underlying health conditions. You could kill them. Never mind that, even young and healthy people are dying from this disease. To my mind, that would make you a murderer. It's reckless negligence. Criminal negligence. There should be a criminal charge for that. People like you should spend your fucking life in jail to pay for your stupidity."

Andrew rose quickly, the color draining from his face. "I see you're not gonna listen to reason, so it's time for me to fuck off."

Jamie also rose, clenching his fists, his face reddening with rage. He stepped toward Andrew, raising a fist.

Andrew backed away.

Jamie lowered his fist, retreated, and sighed. Beating the shit out of Andrew wouldn't accomplish anything. Violence never solves anything. A few blows to Andrew's head would probably only serve to make him stupider than he already was, and that was hard to beat.

"I agree," Jamie said. "It's time for you to fuck off from my garage, and fuck off from my life. Forever!"

***

After Andrew stormed out of the man-cave, Jamie listened for the sound of his car starting, just on the off chance that he might grab a baseball bat from his trunk and return to level the playing field. Jamie was a much bigger man than Andrew. Jamie heard the sound of Andrew's car start, the revving of a cold engine, and then Andrew sped out of Jamie's cul-de-sac.

Good. The fucker is gone. But Jamie's temper flared again. He slammed his meat hook of a fist into the wall of his man-cave. It went right through the drywall and was stopped by a wooden stud.

"Oww," Jamie said, retracting his fist from the hole in the wall and examining his hand. Not even a scratch, just a few drywall chips and drywall dust. He rubbed the throbbing pain away and plunked himself down on the couch, instinctively reaching for another beer. Ten months into the pandemic and he realized, not for the first time, it was taking a toll on his mental and physical health. The loneliness. The sadness. Yes, even the depression. It all led to a very short fuse and a hair-trigger bullshit meter.

During this most recent lockdown, the measures mandated only leaving home for essential services, limiting and not expanding your social bubble, and essentially self-isolating for a month. The beers with Andrew. Well, that could be explained away. Andrew had said he had to get some antihistamines at the pharmacy for his allergies and on the way home he would stop in for a few beers. Whether that was true or not, Jamie now had his doubts. But it didn't matter much now, did it? Andrew was here and gone, and gone for good.

And that meant Jamie's social bubble had now effectively been reduced to zero. Even though Jamie was 53, his other friends were of the elderly and underlying-health-condition variety. Out of an abundance of caution and an unwillingness to risk inadvertently infecting them, Jamie hadn't seen Thelma, Aldo, Patrick, or Theo for over ten months.

He sighed, sipping his beer. Maybe at one point in his life he would've had more patience for lame-brained conspiracy theories, but not now. Times were much different now and, even with the vaccines now being administered, life as we know it would probably never be the same again. How could he say nothing when Andrew was running around like a chicken with his head cut off probably infecting everyone he came into contact with?

Wait a second! That means he could've infected me. Never mind, don't go down that rabbit hole. You didn't know he was behaving so recklessly until today. And I acted on it and kicked him the hell out of my house and the hell out of my life.

Even with the vaccine, Jamie believed things would get much worse before they got better. Anti-maskers, anti-vaxxers, conspiracy theorists, and freedom-fighting idiots were publicly demonstrating en masse around the world, many in defiant violation of lockdown measures. The results were always the same. Violence. Murder. Arrests. A few weeks later, massive COVID-19 outbreaks—many resulting in death—among the demonstrators and their victims.

"Don't think about it," Jamie said, tossing his half-full beer in the garbage can. "It will only make you depressed like it always does, and you won't be able to sleep."

He turned off the man-cave furnace, flicked off the light, and went through his attached atrium and into his house. He had to do something, anything to take his mind off COVID-19. What did the shrinks recommend? Take your COVID news in small doses. Find distractions. Projects. Exercise. Get a routine. Keep yourself busy. Connect with your friends digitally if you can... blah, blah, blah.

He plunked into his living room sofa, ran a hand through his shortly cropped gray hair, and picked up the TV remote. After a moment's thought, he put it down and picked up his cellphone. He hadn't spoken to 87-year-old Aldo in months. Jamie was a muscle car nut and Aldo had helped him rebuild a 1969 Dodge Charger five years ago and their friendship had flourished organically from there. He'd since sold the Charger and had purchased a 1964 Ford Mustang nine months ago that now sat in his garage, collecting dust, collecting rust.

It was early still. He wasn't that drunk. What, four beers? Something like that. He dialed Aldo's number and got him on the first ring.

"Hey, buddy, how are you?" Jamie said.

"I'm okay." Aldo's voice sounded weak, his tone, sad.

"Are you sure?"

"No, actually, I'm not sure."

"Why? What's wrong?"

"I just tested positive for COVID."

"Fuck!"

***

Andrew didn't think a stop at his elderly mother's house was unwarranted. Glenda had always leant a sympathetic ear when he needed her emotional support. Besides, she was an anti-vaxxer and a conspiracy theorist just like himself. She certainly wouldn't be worried about that fucking fake COVID shit. *Not like Jamie, that fuck-up*. Andrew hadn't seen his mother in a few days, he'd been so busy reading, digesting, and believing coronavirus conspiracy theories.

He turned down a tree-lined street in the upscale neighborhood of Lake Bonavista, found her house, and pulled into the driveway. He killed the engine of his black Toyota Camry, exited, and walked up her snow-covered walkway to the house. Usually, she had a snow-shoveling service shovel the sidewalks. Perhaps they too had been affected by the lockdown.

He knocked on the door and waited in the cold for his mother to answer. Although she was 79, she kept herself pretty active and was still quite mobile. Then why wasn't she answering? He rubbed his hands together and tried the door handle. Locked. He knocked again, calling out her name.

"Be right there," a raspy voice said from the other side of the door.

Glenda opened the door and smiled weakly at her son. "Andrew?"

"Mom." He stepped inside and gave her a big hug. He released her and, noticing the dark circles under her eyes and disheveled hair, asked, "How are you?"

She coughed, covered her mouth, and then sneezed into her elbow. "I'm fine, son. Just a little cold. It'll be gone in a day or so. Come in and have some tea."

Sitting in the kitchen sipping tea with his mother, Andrew detailed the explosive argument with Jamie, sugar-coating the profanity, yet telling her in no uncertain terms how it had ended. He was in search of that sympathetic ear, maybe even a fragile shoulder to cry on.

She studied him with matriarchal concern. "He's just another nut-job like so many others. He calls them conspiracy theories. They're not conspiracy theories. They're documented facts."

"I know, Mom. But try telling Jamie that. He freaked out on me and almost punched me in the face."

"Well, he's one stupid son of a bitch. You don't need people like that in your life. Let me tell you the deal with the two vaccines that have been approved by Canada if you don't already know. The Pfizer vaccine, that's the one designed to cull the population. Kill people. The Moderna vaccine, that's a different story. It contains a microchip that will not only allow the government to read your thoughts, but also control you.

Essentially turn you into pawns of the government. It will make you do their bidding obediently and without question. Did you know that?"

"Yes, Mom. I'm a card-carrying member of the resistance."

"Of course you are. Sorry."

"And, speaking of that, I can't stay long. I have a public demonstration to attend this afternoon downtown. It should be interesting."

"I hope it's productive. I hope you're able to recruit lots of people. Show them what a hoax this pandemic really is. Show the world that Alberta has no right to make masks mandatory. Trying to strip us of our civil liberties and freedoms."

"They have no right to lock down the economy either, Mom. They're deliberately catapulting Canada into unprecedented economic woes. Creating a disastrous situation that'll be much worse than the Great Depression. Come to think of it, that might be part of the strategy to cull the population. Kill people by starving them."

Glenda scratched her wrinkled chin, pondering it. "You might have something there. I never thought of that."

After a few minutes of conversation, discussions about the weather, Andrew's career, and Glenda's decision to sell her estate home and down-size to a condo, Andrew rose to leave.

"I'll help you get your house ready to sell when the time comes, Mom." He leaned over and kissed her on the cheek. "In the meantime, I better run."

"Be careful of those pandemic believer protesters," Glenda said. "They're a crazy and dangerous lot."

"I will, Mom. By the way, did you fire that guy who shovels your snow?"

"No. He gave me some cockamamie story that he has COVID."

"Do you want me to shovel your walk before I go?"

"Please. That would be great. I might get a fine from the city if I leave it like that. They do that now, you know. Drive around and ticket people if they don't shovel their walks fast enough. Disgusting. Already trying to control our every move. And wait until this goddamned vaccine gets widely administered."

"See you soon, Mom."

"You promise?"

"Cross my heart and hope to die."

"Good. Keep fighting the good fight, and stay safe."

***

Jamie didn't fully understand why he was torturing himself by watching a live demonstration on the news. The footage showed a large gathering of about 10,000 people surrounded by riot control police on three sides. The demonstrators marched down the middle of a downtown street. With the exception of a few who tried to conceal their identities by wearing black balaclavas, the remainder were not wearing the mandatory protective face masks. Neither were they complying with the mandatory social-distancing—six feet apart—public health measure. Many held placards: THE PANDEMIC IS A HOAX; GIVE US LIBERTY OR GIVE US DEATH; OPEN THE ECONOMY; COVID IS FAKE NEWS; MASK EQUALS GOV'T CONTROL; THE VACCINE KILLS.

"What a bunch of dumb fucks," Jamie said to the TV. "Openly defying public health orders and endangering people's lives. I hope they arrest the fuckers, lock them up, and throw away the key."

So far, violence had not erupted. There were a few fringe demonstrators, pandemic believers, watching the protesters from the sidewalk. All were social distancing. All wore protective masks.

"Go home, you fucking murderers," a man shouted.

"Yeah, go home and we'll go home," a woman said.

A scraggly, blonde-haired man leading the protesters stopped, turned to the pandemic believers, and thrust his middle finger defiantly toward them. "Go fuck yourselves, you brain-washed motherfuckers."

Jamie knew it was only a matter of time before violence erupted. The last protest led by these batshit crazy conspiracy theorists had resulted in ten arrests and seven people injured. One pandemic believer had been beaten so badly he was still clinging to life in the intensive care unit. His prognosis was not good. In similar protests in the United States, some pandemic believers had been murdered.

Jamie's thoughts drifted back to his long-time friend, Aldo. The phone call had been cut short because an ambulance had arrived at Aldo's house to rush him to the hospital. Irene, his elderly wife, suffering from several comorbidities, was also going in for testing. Good chance she would test positive. Good chance she would die. Good chance Aldo would die.

And the worst part of all, due to pandemic restrictions, Jamie would not be allowed to visit his friend in the hospital. None of Aldo's friends or family for that matter would be allowed by his bedside. Maybe Aldo would die alone, lonely, and sad. Perhaps the only exception, Jamie reasoned hopefully, might be if Irene tests positive. Maybe health care workers would take pity on them and put them in a room together—to die together.

What a morbid thought. Don't think like that. Think positive. They'll both recover. Maybe Irene doesn't even have COVID.

However, as much as Jamie tried to derail the negative freight train, he wasn't having a lot of success. He was about to turn the TV off and go read a novel when something caught his eye. A camera man had zoomed in on the leader of the protest, who had grabbed a microphone, stepped onto a makeshift podium, and was about to give a speech.

Jamie had no trouble identifying the man.

It was his one-time friend, Andrew Robinson.

Jamie watched as Andrew tapped the mic, cleared his throat, and began his speech: "We know what's really going on here, don't we, folks?"

Cheers and applause.

"The government manufactured the pandemic to control us; to strip us of our human rights and civil liberties. Governments around the world conspired against us. They created this fake pandemic to scare us. And many people—in fact, the majority of the world population—bought into it. It's not really complicated. Fear sells!"

Cheers and applause.

Riot police, leading with their shields, began closing the gap.

"That's right, fear sells. But we're not stupid enough to buy it. We're here to safeguard our rights, to show the world that we have the freedom to live our lives how we damn well please. No, we're not going to buy into the bullshit pandemic. Nor will we buy into the vaccines. We know what the vaccines really are. Some are designed to kill us; others, to read our thoughts and control us."

Cheers and applause.

Riot police marching closer and closer.

"But we're not gonna let that happen, are we?"

Voices chanting in unity: "No we're not, we'll stop the plot!"

As riot police tightened the noose, Andrew pointed a finger at them. "Leave us alone. You can't stop freedom of speech, and the freedom to demonstrate peacefully. It's enshrined in the Canadian Charter of Rights."

One of the helmeted cops stood in front of his troops. He raised a bullhorn to his mouth, and lifted his face shield. He turned the bullhorn on. It screeched static for a second before he addressed the crowd: "Please disperse now. This is an illegal demonstration. If you don't disperse immediately, you will leave us no choice but to start making arrests."

A demonstrator tossed a beer can at the cop. It arced through the air and struck him on the side of his helmet. Another demonstrator threw a rock that hit the cop square in the forehead. He dropped the bull horn and dropped to the pavement.

Raucous applause erupted from the demonstrators.

Two cops rushed to the injured cop's side and helped him to his feet. He retrieved the bullhorn. Blood dripped down his forehead.

"I said disperse immediately," he said.

"You disperse immediately," Andrew taunted. "Get the hell out of here and let us exercise our civil rights in peace."

A tear gas canister soared through the air and landed next to Andrew. It began hissing white gas clouds. He coughed, covered his face with a hand, stepped off the podium, and retreated. A balaclava-clad demonstrator standing behind him raced over to the spewing tear gas canister, picked it up, and lobbed it at the riot police.

Pandemonium erupted. More tear gas. Riot police moved in, some tackling demonstrators to the pavement. Screaming and shouting. People dispersing en masse. Demonstrators being cuffed and hauled off to waiting police vans.

Through the mayhem, Jamie saw Andrew weaving his way through the crowd in full retreat mode, running like the scared little puppy dog he was.

"I hope they fucking catch you, lock you up, and throw away the fucking key, you chicken-shit piece of shit," Jamie said, waving an angry fist at the TV.

But the scene became too overwhelming and he turned the TV off. Here he was trying to cheer himself up and he was working himself into a hatred-and-rage-filled frenzy. And he realized. Harboring hatred only destroys the haters. Like an aggressive cancer, it eats you up from the inside out and eventually swallows you whole—devastating you both physically and mentally. Turning you into an angry, cynical, and unhappy son of a bitch.

It was bad enough the trauma spawned by the coronavirus pandemic was kicking the crap out of him as it was. He didn't need to add insult to injury. He wandered into the kitchen. Even though he'd lost his appetite, he decided some comfort food was in order. He'd force it down if he had to in an effort to cheer himself up. He opened the fridge and took stock of his supplies. A dozen or so beers. An open can of beans. Some week-old leftover pizza, probably petrified rock by now. A few condiments. A jar of pickles. Not much else. He opened kitchen cupboards to a similar story and decided it was high-time to do some grocery shopping.

About a half hour later, packing a grocery list, hand sanitizer, and protective face mask, he weaved his way through late-afternoon traffic on his way to the grocery store.

After finding a parking spot in the parking lot, he sighed when he saw the lineup. Late afternoon in late November and it seemed everyone wanted to go grocery shopping at the same time. *Never mind. Take your place in line and shut the fuck up.*

***

Andrew managed to scramble to his vehicle just as he heard shouts and screams behind him. Pulling his keys from his pocket in a panic, he wiped his tear-stained eyes and coughed. He looked back and saw Marnie Thompson being tackled to the sidewalk by two cops. One of the key members of the resistance who Andrew had indoctrinated and promised to protect, he couldn't care less about her now. Self-preservation was the overriding concern. It was every man for himself.

"Andrew, help," she said as a cop drove a knee into her spine and began cuffing her.

Ignoring her plea, he quickly unlocked his car door, climbed in, started it up, and drove off, taking the first right turn he saw and hoping the cops hadn't recorded his license plate number. He knew sometimes these investigations could last for months, and just when you least expected it, you could get a knock on your door, only to answer it and have some asshole cop arrest you, cuff you, and start reading you your Miranda rights.

He was about to head toward his downtown apartment but changed his mind. As a result of the demonstration, there would be too much heat in the downtown core right now. A better bet would be to hit suburbia and wait it out for a few hours before attempting the trip home.

To kill some time, he decided to head to the grocery store. The Calgary Coop where he sometimes shopped also had a liquor store next to it and he could kill two birds with one stone.

***

It had taken almost an hour, but Jamie was now close to the front of the line. Third from the front actually. A white-smocked woman wearing a mask stood just outside the sliding-glass doors. She held a clip board, jotting down numbers, and keeping track of how many people entered and how many people left. Due to the pandemic, the grocery store was operating at a third of its customer capacity.

The people standing in line were spaced six feet apart and all wore masks. The bone-chilling temperatures had scared off a few would-be shoppers and the line had dwindled from about thirty people to only about ten now.

"Put your mask on," an angry voice behind Jamie said loudly.

He turned around and saw a large grizzled man pointing a finger at a skinny man about half his size. They stood at the end of the line.

"I don't have a mask," the smaller man said.

"Then fuck off," the big man said. "Masks are mandatory. Where the fuck have you been?"

"I'm outside. I don't need a mask outside."

The big man advanced toward the smaller man.

Jamie squinted. *Fuck, no.* Even in the crimson light of dusk, he recognized the man at the end of the line.

Andrew Robinson.

His mind raced. Should he intervene? At 187 pounds and almost six feet tall, sure he was bigger and more muscular than Andrew. But this Grizzly Adams confronting Andrew easily stood six-foot-five and must have topped the scales at a gargantuan 280 pounds. Jamie doubted he'd stand a chance, not to mention he didn't much like his former friend Andrew right now. After all, he'd just kicked him out of his man-cave and out of his life. In no uncertain and profanity-laden terms to be precise.

The argument continued, their voices growing louder and more agitated. Grizzly closed the gap to within three feet from Andrew. "If I say you need a fucking mask, you need a fucking mask. You got a problem with that?"

Andrew stepped back, but his next words only threw fuel on the fire. "Yeah, I got a problem with that. I got a problem with you as well. If I decide not to wear a mask, that's called freedom of choice, and it's enshrined in the Charter of Rights..."

Andrew would've said more, but Grizzly didn't give him a chance. He quickly closed the gap, grabbed Andrew by the throat with both hands, and lifted him high in the air.

"Put... put me down," Andrew gasped.

"Fine then," Grizzly said, tossing Andrew hard to the pavement.

Andrew landed on his back and then his head smacked the pavement. He lifted his head, moaned, and tried to stand up.

Grizzly, however, had a different plan. He stepped forward and kicked Andrew hard in the ribs.

Jamie didn't even have to think about what he would do. Maybe it was instinct. He didn't know. But he left his place in line, raced to the end of the line, and grabbed Grizzly by the arm just as he was about to deliver another kick to Andrew's head.

Grizzly spun around, surprised the smaller man would have the gall to come to this clown's defense. Hell, even Jamie was surprised by his own actions.

"What the fuck do you want?" Grizzly said.

"He's had enough," Jamie said. "You made your point. Leave him alone. Please."

Andrew, meanwhile, was curled up on the ground gasping for breath.

"If he's not gonna wear a mask, one of two things is gonna happen," Grizzly said. "Either I'm gonna kick the fuck out of him, or he better fuck right off right now."

"I'll get him out of here," Jamie said. He then bent down and began helping Andrew to his feet.

Grizzly stepped back, noticed the line moving, and reclaimed his place in it.

"You?" Andrew said. "What're you doing here?"

"Never mind," Jamie said. "Let's get you to your car. You need to shop somewhere else today. And when you do, make sure you're wearing a fucking mask."

A few cars had already stopped in front of the action and, of course, the few people in the lineup were enjoying ringside seats. Some spectators grinned; others filmed it on their smart phones.

"I think that fuck broke a couple of my ribs," Andrew said, as Jamie found a narrow opening between two cars and helped him through it.

"He would've done more than that if I didn't show up," Jamie said. "Where's your car?"

Andrew pointed. "You're right. Thanks for that."

"Sounds like a lot of people are telling you to fuck off today," Jamie said. "Even the cops."

They'd arrived at Andrew's Toyota. One part of Jamie wanted to slam Andrew face-first on the car hood and take over where Grizzly had left off. Instead, Jamie released Andrew and watched him fumble around in his pocket for his keys, pressing his other hand tightly against his ribs and wincing in pain.

Andrew put his key in the driver's door keyhole and turned to Jamie. "You saw the protest? You were there?"

"I watched it on TV."

"We're doing the right th—"

Jamie stepped back and removed his facemask, running a hand through his short gray hair. "The fuck you are. I don't wanna talk about your fucking conspiracy theories. Not now. Not ever."

Jamie turned to leave. Five steps later, Andrew called out his name. Jamie turned around. Andrew was inside his Toyota with the engine running and the window rolled down.

"What?" Jamie said.

"Even though we have our differences, thanks for doing that back there. I appreciate it. I owe you."

"You don't owe me a thing," Jamie said, turning and walking away.

Returning to the line, he gave Grizzly a wide berth and moved up to his spot at the front. Fortunately, an elderly woman had saved his spot and gestured for him to step in line. He thanked her, took his place, and searched the parking lot for Andrew's black Toyota. He saw the car weaving through the parking lot. He wanted to make sure Andrew was actually leaving and not returning to cause more trouble. If he did, Jamie thought, he probably *would* take over where Grizzly had left off. He was a hair-trigger away from flying into a rage.

Andrew drove slowly through the parking lot. As he turned to exit, two cop cars pulled in, one blocking the front of his car, the other stopping in front of the driver's-side door. Two cops jumped out of one cop car, drew their guns, and approached the vehicle rapidly.

"Step out of the vehicle with your hands up," one cop said.

"Get out of the vehicle with your hands up," another said. "Now!"

Andrew stepped out with his hands up. One cop moved in, tackled him to the ground roughly, inserted a knee on his spine, and cuffed him. Two cops then lifted him to his feet and practically dragged him to the police cruiser.

As they stuffed him inside, Andrew said, "What'd I do? What'd I do? There's been a mistake. Let me go."

The door slammed shut, silencing Andrew's protests. The cop car containing Andrew sped away. Two cops exited the other cop car and began circling Andrew's vehicle. One made a call, presumably to call a tow truck, Jamie figured.

"That your friend?" asked the elderly woman who'd saved Jamie's place in line.

"No," Jamie said.

"You ask me, he's a loser who deserves what he gets."

***

Ten days later, things had settled down to a dull roar. Jamie passed his time in self-isolation by trying different food recipes, eating junk food, binge-watching thriller movies, watching his daily dose of depressing pandemic news, and doing a little reading when he was able to concentrate. His job site was still shut down, the province of Alberta was still in lockdown, and fortunately, he had qualified for the Canadian Emergency Response Benefit—a federal government bail-out implemented in the wake of the crippling pandemic. He was receiving $2,000 a month to sit on his ass and feel sorry for himself. And, for the most part, he was doing just that.

He hadn't heard from his friend, Aldo. He hadn't called any of his other friends and he'd made no effort to contact his former friend, Andrew. Besides, Jamie had heard that Andrew was rotting in a jail cell right now. Right where he belonged.

Jamie sat on his couch on that Wednesday evening, mindlessly channel-surfing. Even if he wanted to go for a walk, the weather wouldn't permit it. It was brutally cold outside and the weather man was calling for two feet of snow overnight. It was as if Mother Nature had not only decided to wipe out a portion of the human race, She'd also decided that, at least in Calgary and at least for tonight, you will be stuck right the fuck in your house.

"Maybe we deserve it?" Jamie said to an empty living room. "All the fucking damage we've done to the planet, maybe this is Mother Nature's revenge."

Something on TV caught his eye and he stopped channel-surfing.

"This just in," the male news anchor said. "The protest spearheaded by 50-year-old local resident Andrew Robinson in downtown Calgary ten days ago has resulted in a super-spreader event."

"Oh, fuck," Jamie said, dropping the remote. Watching the news in the immediate aftermath of the event, he had learned that 16 people had been arrested and 4 people had suffered minor injuries as a result of the protest. Suffering from pandemic depression and delirium, he hadn't considered the possibility of a super-spreader event.

The anchor cleared his throat and continued: "Through vigilant contact tracing, authorities have discovered at least 76 people who have tested positive with COVID-19 as a result of the protest. While details remain unclear, chief medical officer Linda Mickle believes the transmission started with Robinson's elderly mother, Glenda, who infected her son, who then spread the virus like wildfire at the protest. Seventy-nine-year-old Glenda Robinson passed away yesterday from COVID-19 and at least half a dozen other protestors have died from the virus as well. Andrew Robinson, who is facing a long list of charges in connection with the protest, has been admitted to Foothills Medical Centre. Anyone who has had contact with Andrew Robinson within the last ten days should call..."

Jamie turned the TV off and raced into the bedroom to look for his cellphone. It slowly dawned on him that he'd barely turned it on in the last ten days, he'd been so utterly lost in the pandemic fog.

He located it on a bedside table and turned it on. Sure enough, three messages. One from his mother wishing him well and inquiring about his health. Another from his sister, saying Ontario was in lockdown and she too was going in to get tested for COVID. And another from a Scott Ryerson, a contact tracer for the provincial government's coronavirus task force. Ryerson wanted Jamie to call ASAP. Jamie jotted down the contact tracer's number, sat down on the bed, and dialed it.

He was met with a pre-recorded message saying the agency was closed and informing him of its hours of operation. He hung up, went into the kitchen, and sat down at the table. Worry and fear began to eat him up from the inside out like an aggressive flesh-eating disease. Was he sick? Had Andrew infected him? If so, how many people had he infected? *Shit, shit, shit, shit, shit. Fuck, fuck, fuck, fuck.*

He started writing down the dates and times of his outings since coming into contact with Andrew. Fortunately, due to the lockdown, he hadn't seen any of his friends, nor had he ventured out except for essential tasks. And he'd always taken the proper precautions. Social distancing. Mask wearing. Sanitizing his hands before leaving the house, inside his vehicle before touching anything, and again when he returned home. He'd even gone so far as to sanitize his groceries and all high-touch house surfaces with disinfectant wipes.

His phone rang, fraying already jangled nerves. He checked the number. Unknown. But his curiosity got the better of him and he answered.

"Hello," Jamie said.

A weak, croaky voice: "I'm sorry."

"What?"

"I fucked up. Big time."

Finally, Jamie recognized the voice. "Andrew?"

"Yes. Have you been tested yet?"

"No."

"Are you sick?"

"No."

"Get tested. Please. Has the contact tracer been in touch with you?"

"Yes. I just got his message. I tried to call but they're closed now. I'll try again tomorrow."

"This is probably the last call I'll be able to make," Andrew said. He coughed violently for a few seconds before continuing: "I'm dying, Jamie. They're about to put me on a ventilator to help me breathe. I was so fucking wrong and now

I've killed so many people. I suppose I deserve to die, but I just wanted to say I'm sorry."

"Don't worry about it."

"Oh, but I *am* worried about it." More coughing. "It haunts me. Whatever you do, please take this virus seriously. It's real. It's deadly. It already killed my mother and several demonstrators. Now, it's my turn... to die..."

Andrew trailed off and Jamie heard muted conversation in the background. Probably health care workers preparing to intubate Andrew with a ventilator.

"Andrew," Jamie said, his voice tinged with emotion. He felt his cheeks moisten and wiped his tears away. "I... I forgive you!"

Click!

The line went dead.

I Hate That

"I hate that," Peggy Simpson said to Blair Andreas over a bottle of wine. "When people write lol or use a stupid emoji to express lol."

"Jeez, you hate a lot of things," Blair said. "You hate it when people say, 'It is what it is.' You hate it when people drive too slowly; you hate Christmas; you hate your birthday; you hate watching the news. You hate it when people use lol. And, oh yeah, now you hate your sister. Have I missed anything?"

A shadow passed over Peggy's face. "Yeah. I hate you too."

Blair silently watched Peggy leave. She left not so silently, slamming the door of his one-bedroom apartment on Main Street Murray River, Prince Edward Island.

Ahh, hell. Let her go. Who needs all that negativity? Not me, that's for sure. He poured another glass of wine. Peggy had only finished half of her first glass, so he certainly couldn't blame her ill humor on drunkenness.

His hand gripped the glass with a little too much force. He sighed deeply, trying to calm himself down. No point in getting angry. *What was it Samuel Jackson had posted on social media recently? Right.* It went like this: "Never let anyone define your existence, chart your path, or limit your dreams!"

Why should I let Peggy piss me off? It's her shit, and she should own it. Besides, anger and negativity only infect the people spewing the venom. It destroys them from the inside out, and leaves them unhappy, cynical, angry, and not very fun to be around.

He removed his baseball cap, ran a hand through his mop of curly brown hair, and replaced it. He took another sip of wine and began pondering his short friendship with Peggy. He'd met her at a coffee shop in Murray River about a month ago. They'd started chatting about this and that, and that had led to another coffee shop date where he had learned more about Peggy. She was 38, roughly the same age as Blair. She wasn't bad looking, in a rather plain-Jane sort of way. But neither was he a stud, standing five-foot-fuck-all and sporting a pot-belly, the result of an insatiable sweet tooth. She worked at the grocery store in Murray Harbour, a small nearby town. He worked for a landscaping company and had been laid off for the winter. A native Islander, Peggy had come from a family of four. Blair also had a brother and sister, mother and father, living in Toronto, Ontario.

The second coffee shop date had led to Blair visiting Peggy twice at her house in Murray River. And that had led to a visit over a bottle of wine at Blair's flat. A soiree that had lasted about 25 minutes before her unceremonious exit.

What was Peggy really all about? Maybe she had expectations beyond just friendship, which Blair didn't. A newbie to PEI, Blair had tried to steer clear of the gossip on her. Yet he'd heard a few rumors. It was inevitable living in a small town. Divorced twice. Four children from the unions, none of whom she had custody of. No friends. Unstable.

Initially, he'd ignored the rumors and decided to give Peggy a chance. Treat her with kindness and respect and see if she reciprocated, never mind all the gossip. For the most part, that had happened. Except, slowly, he'd started to notice that

Peggy harbored a lot of negativity and anger. He was beginning to see red flags.

No friends. Seriously, who has no friends? Even Blair, who'd only lived on the Island for two years, had four Islander friends. He knew there were certain Islanders who would not socialize outside of their circle of Islander friends and family. But, his friends, although they weren't yet of the inner circle variety, welcomed CFAs—Come From Aways. Thinking back on his list of friends in Ontario, he tried to remember how many of them had no other friends. *Probably none.* Somewhere along the way, they'd crossed a line and he'd cut them loose. Would the same thing happen with Peggy? Maybe he should've just let her comment about hating lol slide off him like water off a duck's back. *No. It's a sign. A sign of bad things to come. I should get rid of her now, while it's still early in the relationship, and I don't owe her a bunch of excuses.*

Unstable. That little rumor bothered him more now since he'd just watched Peggy say she hated him and then storm out of his apartment. The point he had tried to make, and failed dismally, was that it wasn't healthy to harbor so much hatred. She hadn't given him the chance to finish. And now she hated him. Finishing off his glass of red wine, re-corking the bottle, and putting it in the fridge, he decided it was probably best to leave her alone. Don't contact her. She probably wouldn't call. But, if she did, ignore the calls. And ignore emails. Cut off all communication entirely and move on. Who needs friends full of so much negativity? *They just bring you down. Discard them like yesterday's trash.*

***

The next day—Saturday. Although it was the middle of January, the weather man was calling for another unseasonably mild day. After showering, dressing, eating, and doing a few domestic chores, Blair decided a bit of fresh air was exactly what he needed to help him rejuvenate his mind and soul. He'd woken from a disturbing nightmare about being stalked by a woman who strongly resembled Peggy. He wanted to purge his mind of any traces of it.

He turned on his cellphone and smiled when he realized he had no voice or text messages. He opened his Gmail, deleted a half dozen spam emails, and saw no sign of Peggy. *Good. I don't think she'll contact me.*

Outside, as he locked the door to his apartment, above a gift shop, the sound of footsteps startled him. He spun around, dropping his keys in his haste. Peggy stood on his tiny fire-escape balcony. She was dressed in black, right down to her matching toque. Her eyes looked bloodshot, as if she'd been crying.

Blair wasn't into uninvited guests. He valued his privacy too much and his other friends knew and respected that. *Give her a break. They do that here. She doesn't know you well enough.*

"Hi," she said.

"Hi. You caught me at a bad time. I have some errands to run."

"No problem. I just came by to apologize for my behavior last night. I'm sorry about that."

"That's okay," Blair said. *It isn't.*

"I hope we can still be friends."

"We'll see." *Wrong answer.*

"I hope we can," Peggy said.

And, before Blair could say more—not that he wanted to—she turned and rushed down the metal fire-escape stairs.

Reaching the bottom of the rear stairs, he couldn't help himself from searching the area to see if Peggy was hiding behind one of the garbage cans in the small backyard. Satisfied she wasn't there, he headed to the side entrance leading to the front of the building and Main Street. He heard the clanging of metal and spun around, half-expecting to see Peggy charging with a knife. No. It was just a Tabby cat that had tipped over a metal garbage can lid while foraging for scraps.

He exhaled deeply, realizing for the first time he had been holding his breath. It wasn't even noon, and already he was getting the creeps. What would the rest of the day yield? He walked around the small town for about twenty minutes, at the end of which he was finally starting to feel a little calmer. He hadn't seen Peggy. He checked his cellphone to see if she had called. Nothing. *No news is good news.*

H walked down the road toward Lendyl Ball's shop. Blair had met Lendyl a few weeks after arriving on Prince Edward Island and had become fast friends with him after Lendyl had repaired Blair's pickup a few times for a fraction of what it would've cost at a mechanic shop. As a seasonal landscaper, Blair couldn't afford to pay the big bucks that mechanics charged. He knew Lendyl didn't mind unannounced drop-in visits and the elderly man was a wealth of knowledge regarding everybody, everything, and anything. Blair had a few pointed questions that he wanted to get off his chest.

"Lendyl," he said, peering inside the shop window. "You in there?"

"Come on in," Lendyl said.

Blair entered and saw Lendyl doing an oil change on a lawn tractor. He'd fired up the woodstove and the shop was toasty warm.

"Working again I see," Blair said.

Lendyl finished filling the machine with oil and set the oil container down on a cluttered counter top. He wiped his greasy hands on a rag, adjusted his baseball cap, and scratched his long gray beard.

"They always bring me work," Lendyl said. "Because they know I do it for way less than what a mechanic would charge."

"Keeps you out of trouble," Blair said.

"I know. But I was supposed to be retired decades ago. And I'm working more now than I ever was before I retired."

"At least it keeps you busy."

Lendyl sighed. "I suppose so. But some of this work I'm gonna start turning down."

Blair had heard that story before. He didn't think it would happen. Lendyl was too charitable to refuse to help someone, unless of course they turned high-maintenance and started giving him grief.

And that thought reminded Blair why he'd stopped by. "Do you know a Peggy Simpson?"

"I know her to see her. I know of her. But I don't have much to do with her. Why?"

Blair explained what had happened during Peggy's recent visit and Peggy's surprise arrival at the doorstep of his apartment that morning. "I'm just starting to get a bad feeling about this. I mean I've heard some of the gossip—unstable and no friends—but I don't like to rely on gossip to make a judgment. I don't know, maybe I should. What do you think of her?"

"I don't know her. I can only tell you what I've heard."

"Please do."

"She's a bit of a strange one. Keeps to herself most of the time. I can confirm that she did lose custody of her kids—two from one marriage and two from another."

"Why is that?"

"I guess a judge determined she was an unfit mother."

"You mean abusive?"

"Not from what I've heard. More like neglectful."

"That could mean anything. Maybe her exes just had an axe to grind."

"Maybe and maybe not."

"There's something you're not telling me."

"Yes, there is," Lendyl admitted. "Her last husband, Reinhold Peterson, told me she tried to drown him in the ocean last summer."

"Really? What happened?"

"See this here lawn tractor?"

"What does that have to do with anything?"

"It's Reinhold's tractor. He just dropped it off yesterday for an oil change and belt replacement. And that's when he told me she tried to drown him."

"That's kind of strange," Blair admitted. "You learn this news yesterday and the next day I come by pumping you for information on Peggy."

Lendyl poked the woodstove fire. When he finished, he put another log inside, closed the door, and turned to Blair.

"Maybe it's coincidentally good timing for you. I wouldn't have much to do with her if I were you."

"You still haven't told me what happened."

"Right. I forgot. I guess they were out on a leisure cruise on Reinhold's speedboat. They stopped somewhere on the water to float around and have a few drinks. Suddenly, out of the blue, she pushes him into the water. Every time he comes up for air, she submerges him again by pushing on his head with an oar. More like hitting him on the head with the oar to hear Reinhold's version."

"How did it end?"

"Apparently, the coast guard showed up."

"They rescued him?"

"No. She saw them and let him grab the oar. Then she pulled him back into the boat."

"Why didn't he press charges?"

"Because of the kids, so he says. Peggy still sees them once a week and he didn't want to deprive them of their mother. I guess he still hopes she'll change. But, from what you say, it doesn't sound like she has."

Blair wasn't sure what he'd been hoping to hear from Lendyl. Maybe he wanted to hear the opposite of what the gossipers were saying. Maybe he wanted to have his worst nightmares confirmed. One way or another, he believed he had to stay away from Peggy. And now more than ever he would have to start watching his back. But, wasn't he missing the one important question?

"Are you okay?" Lendyl asked. "Your face has gone all gray."

Blair struggled to contain his rising panic. "Did Reinhold say why Peggy pushed him into the ocean?"

"Because he rejected her."

***

Arriving at his apartment a few minutes later, Blair was wound tighter than a cuckoo clock. On the way home, he kept glancing back, half-expecting to see Peggy, either in full attack mode, or grinning cynically at him. Neither one of those scenarios materialized.

As he took off his jacket and hung it up on a nearby hook, his phone rang, startling him and almost causing him to drop his keys a second time. He pulled it out of his pocket and checked the number. Sure enough, it was Peggy.

Hell hath no fury like a woman rejected. He answered the phone.

Peggy didn't waste time on social pleasantries. "Listen, Blair, I wanna apologize for my behavior last night."

"Uh, you did that already."

"Yeah, but you didn't say if you forgive me. Do you forgive me?"

"Of course I do."

"Are you sure?"

"Yeah. Why wouldn't I be sure?"

"You didn't look too happy to see me this morning."

"You took me by surprise. I don't like surprise visits."

"I'm gonna come over now."

"I'm sorry, you can't do that. I'm busy now."

"But you are home?"

She probably already knows the answer to that. Did she watch me come home? "Yes."

"What're you doing now that's so important? More important than me?"

Blair paused, wracking his brain for an excuse. "I have to... I have to clean my apartment."

"You got lots of time to do that. You're off work for the winter. Remember?"

"Listen, Peggy, right now is just not a good time. Okay?"

A long pause. A sulking tone. "If you say so."

"If I wanted to visit you one day, and you told me it's not a good time, I would respect that. Respect your right to privacy and your right to decide who you want to see and when you want to see them. All I'm asking is for you to have the same respect for my rights as I have for yours."

"That's fine. I get it. I just wanted to talk. If you don't have time for me I understand."

"Not right now."

"When then?"

"I'm not much for making plans. I find when I do they always go to hell in a handbasket. We'll see."

"Are you blowing me off?"

Truth be told, yes, Blair was trying to blow her off. But this woman wouldn't take no for an answer. How was he gonna get rid of her? In spite of his reservations about offending a potentially volatile woman, he found himself getting angry. And scared. And when those two emotions collided simultaneously, the result was often brutal honesty.

"Listen, if you wanna be my friend, you'll have to respect my rights and my privacy. With all the negativity I've heard lately, I don't know if I even wanna be your friend. But I'll tell you one thing: This isn't a good foundation to start a friendship."

Fortunately, Peggy backed down. "If you wanna be like that I'll let you go then. Have fun with those dust bunnies. Call me if and when you feel like it."

Click!

Blair immediately went around to every window in his apartment and closed all the blinds. He triple-locked the back door, securing a latch, handset lock, and deadbolt. He then dimmed all the lights and paced his small apartment, replaying the conversation over and over again in his mind; trying to decide where he'd fucked up, why he'd fucked up, and if he'd fucked up badly enough to put Peggy on the attack. Certainly, one thing had become abundantly clear. This woman was volatile, unstable, and maybe just a little bit crazy. Was she capable of murder? Did she have the motivation to kill Blair? *I just fucking rejected her, didn't I?*

That last thought was far from comforting.

Maybe some comfort food would fix that. He prepared a cup of tea and a slice of pumpkin pie and sat down at the kitchen table, sipping and picking away at the pie. He'd lost most of his appetite but forced it down anyway.

Thoughts about what to do about Peggy returned with a vengeance: *Should I block her phone number? No, that'll just magnify the rejection and probably make it worse. Should I block her email? No, that'll likely produce the same result.* Eventually, he realized there wasn't much he could do at this point. Other than ignoring her, and that would probably yield the same result as the aforementioned blocking scenarios. But, nevertheless, he decided to do just that. Leave well enough alone and see what happens. Sounded like a lame defense to be sure, but it's not like Blair was getting any epiphanies right now.

He finished the pie and tea, put the dishes in the sink, and decided a nap was in order. The whole ordeal had been emotionally draining and at the very least he needed to recharge before he could come up with a plan, if there was even a plan to be had.

Lying in bed, blinds fully closed, he started to realize the extent of the terror Peggy had already rained down on him. She was probably turning into a stalker. Even though it was early in the game, Blair was already severely rattled. He felt like a prisoner in his own house and began to wonder how others who had suffered, or were suffering, similar fates had faired. *Unless you've gone through it, you can't fully understand it. Unless you've experienced it, you can't fully sympathize with it.*

The sound was distant at first and he thought it was his mind playing tricks on him. But, no, sure enough, his phone, which he'd set on the living room coffee table, was ringing.

"It better not be her," he said, flying into the living room in a rage. "It better fucking not be her."

Of course... it was.

***

A day of enlightening religious worship for some, Sunday morning brought renewed feelings of dread and unease for Blair. Seeing Peggy's incoming call last night, he'd ignored it and let it go to voicemail. She hadn't left a message. Neither had she left messages the other two times she'd called that evening. *Fine with me. No message. No return call.* Not that he would've returned the calls had she left messages. It was just a half-hearted attempt at justifying his actions.

Coffee in hand, he approached the back window of his apartment and studied the small fire-escape balcony. About six inches of snow had fallen overnight and he almost expected to see footprints on the balcony. He sighed, relieved when he didn't see any footprints.

He went into the living room, was about to sit down, and then heard a loud knock on the door.

"What the fu—"

"Hey, it's only me," Lendyl said, his bushy head peering in the tiny window.

Blair's momentary relief was immediately replaced by panic. Lendyl never dropped by unannounced. He must have some news. Bad news.

He opened the door and Lendyl remained standing outside.

"Sorry to drop over unannounced," Lendyl said.

"Don't worry. I do it to you all the time. What's up?"

"I wouldn't have come if I didn't think it was important."

"What's up?"

"Have you heard from Peggy?"

"Yeah. She called me after I got home from your shop yesterday. I talked to her briefly. Then she called three more times last night. I didn't answer those calls. No messages either. Why, Lendyl? What the hell's going on? Tell me what's going on?"

"Get your boots on and grab a jacket. Let's go for coffee in Montague. I wanna be in a public place when I tell you this."

***

Tim Horton's had the usual Sunday crowd, young and old alike sipping coffee, munching on donuts, and regaling each other with stories of their weekend adventures. Lendyl and Blair managed to get a booth, albeit not a very private one.

"Here's the deal," Lendyl said, getting right to the point. "Reinhold came by last night to pick up his lawn tractor. He said he thought he saw Peggy stalking around his house last night. I guess he yelled out to her and she disappeared in the bush, so he couldn't be sure."

"Could be nothing," Blair said, unconvinced of his own words.

"That's what I thought. But then this morning I get a visit from Theodore, Peggy's other ex. Those two are really estranged and I don't even think he lets her see the kids. He brought this fucking gas-powered weed whacker over. I hate working on those things. Anyway, he tells me he saw Peggy's red Ford Taurus cruising back and forth past his house last night. He even called the cops, not that it amounted to much."

"Jesus," Blair said, then lowered his voice, realizing he was in Bible Central. "She must be really desperate."

"Either that or she's completely lost her mind. If everyone, including you, is rejecting her, who knows what she's capable of?"

"So you came to warn me?" Blair said.

Lendyl nodded. "I couldn't live with myself if I didn't and something happened. And I didn't want to do it over the phone, or even in your house for that matter, in case she showed up."

"Maybe I deserve it," Blair said.

"What's that supposed to mean?"

All morning the memory of an incident regarding his ex-girlfriend in Toronto had been scratching at Blair's brain. It had been vague and indistinct, but now it emerged in living color, begging to be released into the atmosphere. No point denying it.

"I had a girlfriend in Toronto. The relationship lasted three years but then I went and fucked it up."

"What, you stalked her?"

"Let me finish."

"Okay. Lower your voice, though. We're attracting eavesdroppers."

Blair moved closer and lowered his voice. "Lenora, my ex, liked being by herself a lot. I didn't understand that about her at the time. One weekend she hadn't returned several of my calls. I started getting panicky and thinking the worst. Something happened to her. She was cheating on me. She wanted to dump me. A hundred different scenarios. Anyway, I finally worked myself up into a complete emotional frenzy and drove to her apartment late at night. I tried calling her from below the apartment but had no luck. She lived on the second floor, above a retail store, kind of like my apartment I guess."

"You tried to break in?" Lendyl asked, worry lines creasing his forehead.

"Not exactly. The entrance to her apartment was on the main floor. But that door was locked and there was no buzzer. I tried knocking a few times and got no response. So I scaled the rear fire-escape steps and ended up pounding on her bedroom window."

"That wasn't too bright."

"I know. Rejection can bring on bizarre reactions in people. I've learned that the hard way."

"So what happened after that?"

"She didn't answer the knocks on the window but eventually the cops did. I guess she was terrified and called the cops. Long story short, when they got me in front of her, she identified me as her boyfriend and they let me go without even writing it up or charging me. When they left, she let me in her apartment for a short time, but then kicked me out again."

"You left quietly?"

"Yeah. I could see I'd scared the hell out of her and regretted it terribly."

"I'm guessing it didn't end well."

Blair frowned, his eyes moistening. "No. It didn't. She dumped me a few days later. I'll never forget the words she used to describe me and my behavior that night."

"What did she say?"

"She called me volatile, unstable, and maybe just a little bit crazy. Exactly the same words I've been using to describe Peggy."

"I can't condone your behavior," Lendyl said. "It was stupid. But you're nothing like Peggy. You didn't start stalking her after that, did you?"

"No. I respected her wishes and stayed the hell out of her life."

"How long ago was that?"

"Almost two years ago. I moved here after that. Lenora and I had a lot of mutual friends. But after that, err, incident, they all sided with her and blew me off. Thought I was some sort of demented stalker. So I can identify with what Peggy must be going through. On some level, I can't help feeling sorry for her. I can't help thinking that maybe I should stop thinking how I'm thinking and just reach out to her. Maybe that's what she needs right now. Does that sound so wrong?"

"I don't think it's necessarily wrong, neither do I think it's wise."

"Really? I mean I didn't fully understand how badly I terrorized Lenora until this shit happened to me—the shoe on the other foot. It's a karmic wake-up call."

"Karma's a bitch when she tears you a brand-new asshole," Lendyl said.

***

The stalker stalking the stalker.

That's what it felt like, Blair thought, parked half a block down from the residence of Reinhold Peterson, one of Peggy's ex-husbands. It was late Sunday, a drizzly January evening in the small town of Murray River. If Blair hadn't taken Lendyl's advice to stay away from Peggy seriously, he certainly *had* taken his advice to himself seriously: *Don't reject a woman in desperate need of acceptance. Help her.*

Maybe it was the sudden compassion and empathy he started feeling after realizing exactly what she must be going through. He'd experienced it on some level himself, after all, when Lenora had dissed him. The anxiety. The fear. The sadness. The madness. He wasn't exactly sure what the reason for his 180-degree turn was. But a few hours after leaving Lendyl, he'd called Peggy twice and left messages; both of which had gone unanswered. Undeterred, he'd driven around Murray River hoping to find her, even passing by her house twice.

Now, here he was sitting in his truck at a quarter to midnight with a pair of binoculars trained on the front porch of Reinhold's small two-story home on a quiet tree-lined street. He thought he saw some movement on the front porch, but a closer look revealed a cat had leaped up on Reinhold's porch railing and was eyeballing the door, obviously wanting to be let in.

Blair was momentarily blinded by the glare of headlights reflecting off his rear-view mirror. He threw the binoculars on the passenger seat and ducked. As the vehicle passed, he slowly raised his head above the dashboard and saw, yes, a Ford Taurus pull in and park across the street from Reinhold's house.

The driver's door clicked open and someone—even in the dim glow from the nearby streetlight, fitting the general description of Peggy—got out and began walking across the street, toward Reinhold's house.

What the fuck am I doing here? But the thought was fleeting. Blair was in far too deep now to change his mind. He grabbed his flashlight, opened the door, and ran towards the person crossing the street. Nearing, he realized it was Peggy.

She stopped in the middle of the road, startled.

"Peggy," he called out. "Don't do that. It's not gonna end well."

"What the fuck are you doing here?" she said. "Stay away from me, you pot-bellied pig!"

He stopped within a few feet of her. "Come on, Peggy. Follow me home and we'll talk. You can't stay here. If he sees you, he's gonna call the cops again."

"What do you mean *again*?" she asked, squinting in anger. "How do you know he called them the first time?"

"I just wanna help you," Blair said, stepping forward and touching her shoulder gently. "Let's get outta here now."

She jerked away swiftly, spun around, and headed toward her vehicle. Opening the door, she glared at Blair. "You had your chance to help me and you fucked it up. Now I hear you're talking behind my back and bad-mouthing me."

"No, that's not true. I just wanted to figure out what was going on. I want to help you. I know how you feel. I used to be like you."

"Doesn't look like much has changed." She pointed to the house. "As a mother, I have the right to see my kids and that fucker is trying to deny me my rights. I'll teach him."

"Not here, not now," Blair said. "We'll work it out. I promise."

"Fuck you," she said, climbing in her car and slamming the door.

As she started it, Blair raced back to his truck. He climbed in and started it as Peggy pulled out and drove away. By the time Blair had pulled out, she'd already reached the end of the street and was turning left.

"Fuck," he said. "She's gonna do something crazy. I just know it."

As he passed Reinhold's house, he saw a man standing on the porch with a cellphone pressed to his ear.

He sped up and caught sight of Peggy's car just as she turned onto Murray's River's Main Street. He managed to secure a safe following distance. She turned toward Murray Harbour and so did he. Blair followed her into Murray Harbour. She drove through the small town and made a left turn toward Beach Point and Cape Bear Lighthouse.

About fifteen minutes later, Blair realized his worst nightmare was coming true. She turned onto the gravel entrance road to the lighthouse and accelerated. He wrestled with his Chevy truck to try and keep it steady, trying to close the gap, hoping to cut her off and force her to a stop. As he got up alongside her vehicle, she wrenched the wheel, side-swiping his truck and sending it careening toward the ditch. Blair gripped the steering wheel hard and wrenched it right as it fish-tailed for a few seconds before finding purchase.

"What the fuck are you doing?" he said, even though he knew she couldn't hear him. He retreated to a safer following distance as she barreled toward the lighthouse entrance. In earlier sightseeing trips around the Island, Blair was aware of the topography of the land on which the lighthouse stood—a seventy-five-foot cliff above the ocean. Surely she wasn't planning on crashing the surrounding metal fence and driving her vehicle off the cliff. *Are you stupid? That's exactly what she's planning.*

Peggy crashed through the frost fence entrance gate. The doors swung open and Blair knew it was now or never.

He floored it and circled her vehicle in a wide arc, coming around to the passenger side as she headed for the cliff. About a hundred feet from the edge, he rammed her passenger door and sent her vehicle spinning in circles as his pickup careened to one side and smashed into a picnic table, shattering it before spinning a complete circle and coming to a stop. He heard a loud pop and realized debris from the picnic table had blown one of his front tires. *Front right. Shit.*

He climbed out of his truck and watched, horrified as Peggy's Taurus careened toward the edge, spinning helplessly out of control. He ran toward the edge of the cliff as the rear end of her car careened over the edge. He heard a loud scraping sound as he approached. The vehicle had caught something—a large boulder maybe—that had prevented it from going over.

The motor revved. The rear tires spun. The car dangled dangerously on the edge—a four thousand pound deadly teeter-totter, swinging back and forth, back and forth.

"Peggy, no," Blair said as he reached the Taurus and pulled open the driver's door.

Her head was slumped over on the steering wheel, both hands still gripping it tightly. He unclasped her seatbelt and heard a soft moan as he dragged her to safety.

A split second later, Blair heard a terrifying metallic scraping sound. He watched the vehicle slide over the precipice and disappear, followed by a crash and a thunderous boom as the Taurus exploded, lighting up the night sky with an eerie orange glow.

Infused with a strong dose of adrenaline, Blair grabbed Peggy's arms and shook her. "Are you okay? Are you okay? Say something. Please."

She opened her eyes slowly.

She grinned.

He released her.

She sat up, reached behind her back, and pulled out a handgun. Pressing the barrel into her ear, she said, "We have to stop meeting like this."

Then she pressed the trigger.

You'll Pay

"You obviously don't get it," Ranse Spilling said. "If you disrespect Mother Nature, you'll pay."

"Like fuck I will," Devon Papilla replied, climbing into his pickup, and driving off.

Ranse was left by himself to examine the carnage. He'd recently hired Corning Excavation to cut a logging road through his 60 acres of woods. It was to be a mile-long road that looped around his property, allowing him easier access to firewood, not to mention the recreational opportunities it would provide. Corning's estimate of $20,000 was the cheapest of three estimates. A few friends on Prince Edward Island had raved about the company's work, particularly Corning's respect for Mother Nature. Since respect for Mother Nature had been foremost on Ranse's mind, he'd hired the contractor. He was already out of pocket $10,000, since Corning had demanded half up front.

However, in spite of the rave reviews and lowest estimate, Ranse didn't like what he was looking at. Two hundred feet of the road had already been cut using a tree harvester, a massive machine. And Devon, a new employee at Corning, hadn't followed Ranse's instructions at all. Instead of piling the timber in a neat pile in a small clearing Ranse had created, Devon had simply tossed them off to the side of the road—right into the thick forest.

Ranse frowned, studying a treed area beside the road where Devon had cut down and dumped three large spruce trees. All of them were pinning down younger, smaller trees, struggling for sunlight and space to flourish in the forest. Ranse saw that a few of the smaller trees had snapped from the weight of the spruce trees—quite literally beheaded.

Grinding his teeth, his eyes wandered to an area beside the downed spruce trees. Devon had piled a bunch of loose twigs—logging slash—into a large pile, right on top of a small grove of white birch trees. Ranse had specifically told Devon to find small openings in the forest and put the slash there—instructions that had been completely ignored.

Ranse's middle-aged forehead knotted with wrinkles and reddened with rage. "Motherfucker, you'll pay. You'll see."

Belinda the blue jay squawked, flew down, landed on Ranse's Gator, and looked at him quizzically.

"I know, Belinda. He's wrecking your habitat." Ranse dug into his pocket and produced a peanut. He tossed it on the ground beside The Beast, as he referred to his side-by-side all-terrain vehicle.

Belinda swooped down, snatched up the peanut, and flew away into the trees, chirping a Thank you before she disappeared.

The distraction went some way to cheering up Ranse; but after five more minutes of surveying the sloppy road-building effort, he was furious again. So he climbed in The Beast and blasted home. As soon as he arrived, he called John Corning, the owner-manager of Corning Excavation. His secretary patched him through right away.

Ranse bit his tongue in an effort to control his temper. Lashing out at John would not produce the results he wanted.

"John?"

"Ranse, how are you?"

"I've had better days."

"What's up?"

"We agreed where to put the slash and where to pile the downed trees. Devon's making a fucking mess out there."

After a pause, John said, "He's not putting the logs or the slash where you want them?"

"Not even close."

"Well, Devon's new, so I'll have a talk with him. But I think you realize that tree harvesters sometimes make a bit of a mess of the forest. With a 22-ton machine, it's not always possible to put things where you want them. If you wanted a less impactful road build, you might have considered another logging method."

Ranse knew John had a point. He'd thought about hiring a couple of chainsaw operators and helping them drop the trees. Precision logging. For sure it would've been less damaging. But he'd seen Corning Excavation build roads in an ecologically sensitive fashion using a tree harvester and a bulldozer to remove the stumps. *But that was Mac, another operator*, Ranse thought. A self-proclaimed tree hugger, Mac prided himself on his operational efficiency; some would call it talent.

"Do you have another operator?" Ranse asked. "Devon is sloppy. What happened to Mac?"

"Sorry. Mac moved to New Brunswick. He's no longer with us."

"Well, if you could have a talk with Devon, I'd appreciate it."

"I'll do that," John said.

Before Ranse could say more, John blew him off the line, saying he had an urgent call on another line.

Ranse poured himself a coffee and went outside and sat on his back porch, hoping the beautiful fall colors would help him calm down. As he sipped his coffee, he realized there might have been a time when he wouldn't have bothered being so fussy about the forest. But that was a long time ago now. In ten years of harvesting his own firewood, he'd learned a lot about the complex forest ecosystem. Although he realized that the collective body of knowledge on the forest ecosystem only scratched the surface of what was actually occurring, he nonetheless prided himself on his logging methods—light selection harvesting, or selective logging.

Over the years, Ranse himself had become a bit of a tree hugger. Or, as he liked to call it, a self-proclaimed conservationist. He'd planted depleted species like red oak in his forest and marveled at how his logging sites had regrown healthier, more sustainable, and more beautiful than before he'd arrived. He was leaving his mark, leaving his legacy in the forest for generations to come.

A card-carrying member of the Prince Edward Island Woodlot Owner's Association, he'd read extensively on low-impact, ecologically sound forest management practices. And he knew it was a learning curve that just kept on curving. There was always more to be learned. He'd made mistakes, missed his mark with notches and angles, and watched, saddened and horrified, as the falling trees destroyed other trees he'd planned on saving.

He identified only too well with renowned conservationist Aldo Leopold's observations: "One of the penalties of an ecological education is that one lives alone in a world of wounds."

But if Mother Nature sustained too many human-inflicted wounds, Ranse had learned from experience—quite literally hard knocks—that Mother Nature would strike back with powerful, vicious, and deadly force.

While the forest gave life to humankind—air, water, carbon capture, erosion prevention, wildlife preservation, to name a few—Mother Nature also had the power to snatch it away violently in a heartbeat.

His own near-death experiences in the woods had given him a new respect for Mother Nature. A new fear. A deeper and more meaningful understanding, affinity, and love.

But it hadn't always been that way. He remembered early in his logging career. Using the simple philosophy—take the worst and leave the best—one day he'd evidently gone a little too far. About a half hour into cutting up some storm-downed trees, he'd gotten a little sloppy and accidentally killed a few healthy maple saplings. Feeling bad about it, Ranse carried on anyway. A few minutes later, limbing a storm-tilted tree, a branch snapped off and smashed him square in the face. His glasses flew off his head, landing a good thirty feet away. About an hour later, he found them and carried on. Stepping back after making a front-cut, he stepped into a small depression and lost his balance, crashing down hard on his back while still holding a running Stihl MS-361 chainsaw. The chain had come to within inches of slicing his throat. Terrified but undeterred, he carried on. A few minutes later, another fall, another close call. The second fall had been more damaging. The chain landed on his gloved hand, cut through the glove, and gouged a six-inch-long gash in his hand. If it hadn't been for quick reflexes, applying the chain guard on, and stopping the chain, he would've lost that hand. That's when he'd packed it in. Three strikes yer out. Know when to run. Hell hath no fury like Mother Nature scorned.

After that terrifying close call, he learned to be more in tune with Mother Nature's moods, coming to revere Her as an all-powerful goddess. If a logging day started off badly, Ranse would simply pack up his gear, load it into The Beast, and call it quits. Logging was dangerous enough as it was without tempting Mother Nature's wrath.

And that's exactly what Devon had been doing. Ranse had tried to explain to Devon that trees communicate with one another, protect their young, and have an intricate, harmonious, and complex relationship with the other plants and animals of the forest.

Devon's reply had been, to say the least, short-sighted. "Don't worry about it. It all grows back on its own anyway."

At the very least, that ignorant statement suggested that people could go ahead and slash and burn the forest at will with a reckless disregard for conservation and it would all grow back. For hundreds of years, humankind has tried that with dismal and damaging results to the forest ecosystem. But, obviously, there was no point trying to explain to Devon the science behind low-impact, eco-friendly, sustainable forest management. He obviously didn't give a flying fuck.

So Ranse had employed a different tact, realizing he was getting nowhere with the conservationist approach. He simply said that Devon wasn't following his instructions on how the job was supposed to be done. He'd asked him nicely to please put the slash in one spot, the logs in another.

To which Devon had replied, "I'll think about it."

And that's when Ranse had become slightly unhinged. He'd said, "You obviously don't get it. If you disrespect Mother Nature, you'll pay."

To which Devon had responded: "Like fuck I will."

Is that what he really thinks? It wouldn't surprise me at all if he loses an arm. Or even gets killed. He almost deserves it.

Ranse finished his coffee, realizing that replaying the whole thing over in his mind was only serving to depress him. Time to put on some news, read a book, anything to get the disheartening topic off his mind. Since tomorrow was Saturday, his day off from his trucking job, he decided he'd get up dark and early and get to work cleaning up some of Devon's fuck-ups. From experience, he knew that many squashed saplings—as resilient as they were— would pop back up again after he removed the big trees pinning them down.

At least if he was in the forest, he could keep an eye on Devon.

And if that smug little fuck wouldn't listen to him tomorrow, he'd fire his ass and tell Corning to replace him with someone competent.

***

By 8:15 the following morning, Ranse had already bucked up several downed spruce trees, watching with joy as many saplings they'd been pinning down sprang to life as soon as he'd removed the life-threatening timber.

He turned his chainsaw off, admiring one baby balsam fir that had been given new life as a result of his surgical precision.

"Why don't you do that when I'm done?" a voice behind him said.

He turned and saw Devon standing beside his pickup, which he'd parked behind the tree harvester. Wearing a black-and-blue lumberjack shirt, he held a thermos in one hand, a smoke in the other. His black-and-red Budweiser baseball cap was tilted to one side and his stringy brown hair poked out like strands of straw.

Ranse set the chainsaw down, wiped a sweaty forehead, and scratched his two-day chin stubble. "I'd rather save a tree *today*."

"Well, you might be in the way. I don't wanna hit you with a tree." A grin appeared on Devon's pock-marked face, but he wiped it away quickly by drinking from his thermos.

"I'll stay well behind you," Ranse said. "Don't worry about it."

Devon shrugged and headed toward the tree harvester. He turned around just before he arrived. "By the way, my boss talked to me yesterday. Guess you called him?"

Ranse started to feel like a rat. *Never mind. Preserving the forest is more important than some stupid feeling of guilt.* "I just wanna make sure the slash goes where I want it and the downed trees go where I want them. Is that too much to ask?"

"I'll do my best," Devon said.

Ranse considered telling Devin to show some respect for Mother Nature but decided against it. The warning had fallen on deaf ears previously and he wasn't in the mood to start the day off on the wrong foot. Besides, he was feeling a little guilty about his morbid thoughts yesterday—hoping that Mother

Nature would teach Devon a lesson by severing a limb, or even worse, killing him.

"I'd appreciate that," Ranse said. "I understand that clearing a road and sites with a tree harvester isn't exactly precision and low-impact logging. But at least if you stay mindful of how I want the job done, that would help."

Devon grunted, took a drag from his cigarette, and tossed it on the ground, stomping it out with a large booted foot.

That irritated Ranse but he tried not to show it. He would pick it up later.

Devon climbed into the tree harvester and fired it up. He rolled forward with the big machine and Ranse watched as he lowered the large fang-toothed jaws around a large pine tree and gripped it tightly. He heard a whirring sound as the metal cutting disc sawed cleanly through the tree before the jaws of death picked it up and placed it directly onto a small tape-marked clearing.

Ranse noticed one small sapling get pinned down in the process and sighed. It wasn't perfect log placement, but pretty damn close. Besides, he understood that part of sustainable forest management meant playing God with Mother Nature. You decide which trees live and which ones die. And it was documented fact that the bigger the spaces between trees, the healthier the growth. For the indigenous species on Ranse's little piece of the Acadian Forest, he'd read that many foresters and conservationists recommended spacing between trees of five to six feet. If trees weren't so crowded, it meant less competition for sunlight and water, which translated to taller and healthier trees and a more biologically diverse forest. At least that part of the science of sound forest management wasn't in dispute.

Ranse watched Devon cut two more trees and place them neatly on the pile with minimal damage to the surrounding trees. *Good. He's listening to me. That's all I wanted.*

He started up his chainsaw and went to work cleaning up some errantly placed spruce and maple trees, bucking them up into firewood and putting them in out-of-the-way neat little piles. He would leave them in the forest to cure over the winter and return next fall or spring to collect them and stack them in his barn, which by that time would be empty of firewood, or close to it.

For a few hours, Ranse got distracted by his work and just being in the forest. It had rained last night and the morning had brought with it a beautiful fall day, not a cloud in the sky and a balmy 15 degrees Celsius. At least, that was balmy chainsawing weather, since it didn't take long at all to break a sweat with such physically demanding work. He turned off his chainsaw and admired his handy work. He'd just saved two maple saplings by freeing them of their wood loads and he was enjoying the day, the beautiful fall colors, and his life-saving efforts. And the work was progressing smoothly. Mother Nature hadn't snapped back at him angrily, at least not yet. A good sign.

He turned off the chainsaw, set it down in the back of The Beast, and reached for his water bottle. It was approaching noon and his stomach was starting to growl. He'd been on a steady diet of caffeine and water all day and it was time for some sustenance.

About seventy-five feet ahead, he heard the rumbling engine of the tree harvester quit. He climbed into The Beast, started it, and drove to where Devon was working. He pulled up about thirty feet behind the tree harvester, turned the engine off, and climbed out. He saw two trees dropped haphazardly in the forest, but otherwise it appeared as if Devon was taking great pains to follow his instructions.

"I know, I know," Devon said, pointing to the misplaced trees. "I missed the mark there. But I'll scoop them up later and put them in the pile over there. Otherwise, what do you think?"

"I have to admit, I'm impressed," Ranse said. "Good work."

As soon as he said it, Ranse heard a loud creak, the terrifying sound of a tree splitting. He looked up and saw that one of the trees next to a tree that Devon had removed—a partially uprooted leaner—was coming down.

Horrified, he saw Devon reaching for his lunch box, unaware of the threat from the large white pine.

"Hey, watch out," Ranse said, realizing as soon as he said it that Devon probably didn't have time to get out of the way. His adrenaline kicking in, Ranse sprinted toward Devon, tackling him to the ground just as the pine came crashing down behind them. Ranse landed on top of Devon, and when the rumble from the tree tumble subsided, felt his extremities. They were all there, intact and uninjured. He quickly got up, extending a hand to Devon.

"Are you okay?" Ranse said. But saw right away that something was wrong. An errant branch from the falling tree—more like a spear—had scraped across Devon's thigh, tearing his jeans and cutting his leg. The 12-inch-long gash was gushing blood.

"You saved my life," Devon said, trying to stand.

"Stay down," Ranse demanded. "Your leg."

Devon saw all the blood and the color drained from his face. "Fuck. That looks bad."

"Stay there," Ranse said. "We've got to stop the bleeding."

Devon wrapped both hands around the wound and blood squirted between his fingers.

Ranse stepped over the downed pine, which had narrowly missed the tree harvester, and rushed over to The Beast. He reached into a plastic utility bin and pulled out a well-worn clean T-shirt that had been recycled into a rag. He quickly returned to Devon and started wrapping it around the wound, trying to stop the bleeding.

Fuck, he's losing a lot of blood. Fast. How long does it take someone to bleed to death? Five minutes? That's if the hemorrhaging doesn't stop. Either way, I don't have long. When he'd slowed the raging river to a babbling brook, he helped Devon to his feet and began leading him to The Beast, with the intention of driving another seventy or so feet to Devon's pickup and then rushing him to the hospital.

Devon was already groggy and on the verge of passing out. "Where... where are we going?"

"Don't talk," Ranse said. "Don't expend too much energy. I'm taking you to the hospital."

As Ranse neared The Beast, Devon closed his eyes, went totally limp, and dropped to the ground, slipping easily from Ranse's blood-soaked grip.

"Stay with me, Devon," Ranse said, kneeling down and trying to pull him back to his feet. He knew it wasn't gonna be an easy task. Ranse weighed about 170 pounds. Devon, on the other hand, must have weighed about 230 pounds.

Devon opened his eyes and smiled. "So peaceful. Where are we, anyway?"

Ranse heard the sound of an engine and spun around. He saw a silver Ford truck heading toward them. The truck stopped abruptly a few feet in front of them. The driver's door opened and John Corning climbed out. The passenger door opened and another man stepped out, a giant of a man and one of Corning's employees.

Corning assessed the dire situation immediately and motioned to the employee. "Get him in the truck, Rex. Now!"

Ranse stepped aside as the big man bent down, hoisted Devon up like a ragdoll, and single-handedly began loading him into Corning's truck.

"What happened?" Corning said.

"A storm-uprooted leaner came down," Ranse said, pointing at the nearby large pine blocking the road in front of them. "A branch from it slashed his leg."

"Ranse saved my life," Devon said as he was being loaded into the truck. "Tackled me out of the way and made a tourniquet."

"Thank fucking God you were here," Corning said.

His heart pounding furiously in his chest, Ranse watched as Corning climbed into his pickup, negotiated a U-turn, and sped away.

You'll pay. You'll pay. You'll pay. The words echoed hauntingly in Ranse's head as he leaned against The Beast, caught his breath, and waited patiently for the power-boosting effects of the adrenaline surge to fade away. He wondered if Devon would live or die, felt overwhelming guilt for previously wishing the worst, and wondered about the future of his ill-fated logging road and recreation site project.

It took a few minutes before he felt normal enough to return and inspect the accident site. He knew one thing for sure. Today's logging operation was a wrap. He wanted to clear out of the forest and return home as soon as possible before Mother Nature decided that another strike was in order, just to show these ignoramus humans that enough was enough. He bent down and picked up Devon's spilled lunch—three Saran-wrapped sandwiches, a Twinkie, two cans of Coke, a can of beans, a can of creamed corn, and a can opener. He put them into the plastic lunch box, closed it, and began walking back to The Beast. Halfway to The Beast, a horrifying creaking noise stopped him in his tracks. He looked up and saw a standing dead tree slip from its precarious moorings and start falling—right toward him. The tree harvester had disturbed the roots around it and it had decided now was the time to fall. Just as Ranse was about to run for his life, he watched the tree snag in some surrounding healthy trees, their branches hugging it securely and stopping its downward trajectory. It would have to come down another day, Ranse knew, sighing deeply and picking up his pace.

But today is definitely not that day. He climbed into The Beast and drove to Devon's pickup, tossed the lunchbox inside, retrieved the keys and locked it, and drove home, slowly and cautiously.

He realized he'd been right all along. *Push the envelope with Mother Nature and you'll pay. It's just a question of how much.*

Lost

"My name is Chad Manfield," I said. "And I've been lost for as long as I can remember."

"I know your name," dream psychologist Annie Fortini said.

"I know, Doctor Fortini," I said. "It just sounds good."

"Please don't make a joke of this," she said, sliding her black-framed glasses up the bridge of her dainty nose and opening a file. "I'm here to help you. And you can call me Annie."

"Sorry, Annie." I didn't want to get off to a bad start with Annie. I thought she was kind of cute, in a bookish sort of way. And I wanted her help, needed her help badly.

"It's okay. When you say you've been lost for as long as you can remember, are you specifically referring to your nightmares? Or do you feel lost in your personal life as well?"

"I have a good job. I'm a pharmaceutical sales rep. I have a good relationship with my girlfriend, Sally. I have a good relationship with my family. I can count my good friends on two hands, which is more than most people can say, I think."

"That's not exactly what I asked you. On top of all that, do you still feel lost in your personal life?"

"No. I don't think so."

"You don't think you feel lost in your personal life or you know you don't feel lost in your personal life?"

"I don't know."

"That's okay... not to know," Annie said, writing in the file. "It sounds like you're being honest. Now, tell me about these recurring dreams of being lost."

"As I said, I've been having them for as long as I can remember. And always the same theme—being lost. I'm wandering around a strange city trying to find my way back home. Taking all kinds of strange twists and turns and not having a clue where I'm going. Sometimes I'm walking. Sometimes I'm driving. Sometimes I'm running. The anxiety of being lost eventually becomes overwhelming and I wake up. Can you tell me what this means?"

"I can offer you some general truths, but for me to properly diagnose and treat your problem, I can't do that in one session. I need to know more."

"Fair enough," I said. "Tell me the general truths."

"Sure. Dreams about being lost can be a manifestation of anxiety or feelings of inadequacy. They often invoke a feeling of confusion, frustration, and even feeling that you don't fit in. Usually, these dreams stem from a situation in your life that you are feeling anxious about and you believe that you won't find your way out of. For example, a new job where you feel your skills are less than adequate, or maybe a move to a new city where you are anxious about fitting in and making new friends. But your situation is obviously a little different. According to information from our initial consultation, you're established in Vancouver, established in your job, and have stable relationships with your friends, girlfriend, and family. Do you remember the very first time you had a dream about being lost?"

"I think I was ten at the time," I said.

"That's over forty years ago."

"Yeah."

"Do you remember the dream well?"

"Fairly well."

"Tell me what you recall."

"I was in a strange city. Huge city. The vibe felt like a third-world country. Honking horns, bustling traffic, people everywhere. A lot of filth, poverty, and squalor. It felt like I was just plopped down in the middle of this crazy-busy intersection, people and traffic everywhere. I had to run across the street to avoid getting run over by a car. The noise got too intense, so I turned down this side street, thinking I'd be able to find my way back home. It seemed like I walked for hours but just ended up deeper and deeper into the labyrinth of unknown streets. Then this mangy dog saw me and started barking and chasing me. Soon there were hundreds of barking dogs chasing me. Then they caught me and started ripping me apart, tearing the flesh from my body in huge clumps. I finally woke up, screaming, heart pounding, covered in sweat."

"Wow. That does sound nightmarish. Do you recollect what your family situation was at the time? Was it stable?"

"As far as I remember, yes. There was just my mom and dad and my sister in our house. We were a functional, happy, close, and loving family. We weren't dysfunctional if that's what you're getting at."

"I'm not getting at anything," Annie said, taking more notes. "I just want to know. Did you have any pets at the time?"

"No," I said. "Wait a minute. We'd just adopted a German shepherd puppy dog. Rex."

"Well, that might explain the dogs in your dream. But that only represents a fraction of what's going on here. Did you experience any loss at the time of the dream? A loss for which you weren't able to process the emotions perhaps?"

"I don't think so."

"Okay. Let's fast forward to the here and now. While dreams are often difficult to study and there's a lot we still don't know about them, usually recurring dreams are a result of your subconscious trying to process areas of stress in your life. The common causes are unfulfilled needs, areas of current frustration, or unresolved issues from the past. I know it's only the beginning, but I don't think yours are the result of unresolved issues. Tell me, do you have any areas of stress in your life right now?"

I wracked my brain. I was generally a happy-go-lucky kind of guy. It was my dreams that were beginning to throw my psyche off kilter. My job was, well, maybe not my dream job, but satisfying enough and certainly financially rewarding. Sally Kimmel was loving and loyal to a fault. I hadn't had any disagreements with friends or family lately. What the hell was wrong with me?

"I wish I could help you," I said, "but frankly nothing really comes to mind."

"Okay. Let's get more specific and talk about unfulfilled needs. Three important needs all human beings have are independence, translated as the need to have a modicum of control in your life. Love, that is the need to love and be loved. And competence, the need to have a meaningful impact on your life and the lives of others. Let's go through these one at a time."

"Okay," I said, doubtful.

"Do you feel you have some control over your life?"

"Yes."

"Are you happy with the amount of control you have, or do you want more?"

"I'm happy with the amount I have." Since she billed out at a hundred and twenty dollars an hour, I wasn't about to lecture Annie about being a law-abiding citizen in a world full of laws, rules, and regulations, many of which I didn't make and I couldn't change.

"Are you happy with the amount of love in your life?"

"Yes. Sally's not my dream girl, but she'll do."

"Hold on. How long have you been with Sally?"

"About six years."

"And she's not your dream woman?"

"No."

"Yet you're happy with the relationship, and in love?"

"Yes," I said. "There's no such thing as a perfect relationship. You're always gonna have to make compromises. Right?"

"That's true," Annie said, but she shot me a skeptical look. "However, if you feel you've settled with Sally and maybe think you deserve someone better, then that could very well be a source of frustration and anxiety in your life. Tell me, do you dream of your dream woman?"

Maybe it's you. "I have, yes."

"And she's obviously not Sally?"

"Correct." *Maybe it is you.*

"What about your career?"

"Well, it's not my dream job, but I like it enough."

"That sounds to me like you think you can do better, but you're settling. I think already you've identified two areas of stress in your life that could be causing these recurring dreams of being lost."

Annie looked at her watch. "Our session is almost over. I have a homework assignment for you. I want you to take two pieces of paper, one for your job, the other for your girlfriend. On each one, write down all the pros and cons of each. That exercise will ultimately tell you if you're dissatisfied with one, or both."

I stood and shook her hand. "Thanks, Annie. I'll do that. Same time next Friday then?"

"Yes... one more thing. I want you to keep a journal beside your bed. In it, I want you to write down all of your dreams as soon as you wake from them. Okay?"

"No problem."

***

Pacing the floor in my high-rise apartment an hour later, I turned over Annie's analysis in my mind, still struggling with the reality that I had two major areas of stress in my life—job and relationship. All this time I thought I was happy. All this time I'd just been complacent and unwilling to think about or address my dissatisfaction issues. Essentially, I'd been living a lie. Or had I?

Was my job so bad? Was Sally so bad?

I decided the only way to find out was to do Annie's exercise. I went into my office, sat down, and pulled two lined pieces of paper out from an upper drawer. On one, I wrote

Sally at the top and made two columns, pros and cons. I titled another one *Job* and decided to start with that one.

At the end of the job exercise, I tabulated both columns. Thirteen pros. Seventeen cons. The biggest con and probably the one that irked me the most was the, *I'd rather be a writer* line. I'd graduated from college with a journalism diploma and then graduated from university with a degree in literature. And here I was selling drugs. Well, at least they were legal. Pharmaceuticals. But my lifelong dream had always been to either be a journalist or a horror author. But, after graduation, I'd gone straight for the bucks. At 55, was it too late for me to change careers?

For the time being, I put it out of my mind and went to work on the *Sally* exercise. A short time later I had a list of sixteen pros and sixteen cons—a tie. I didn't want to believe that Sally and I weren't right for each other. We were both creative, both had sales jobs that under-utilized our creativity. We didn't want to have kids. We weren't interested in the institution of marriage, although we had recently discussed the possibility of living together. At 50, Sally was aging gracefully. She was tall, pleasingly plump, large-breasted, and at least in the eye of the beholder, rather fetching. I'm not a Brad Pitt lookalike, although neither am I a dog's breakfast. I'm a trim 175 pounds, six feet tall, and some of my friends say I look like George Clooney.

Our sex life, well, sure it had waned in the last year or so, but don't they all? I mean how long does that animal attraction or infatuation phase last anyway? We'd managed to milk ours (no pun intended) for at least three years. If you ask me, I'd say that's damned good. Nothing lasts forever, especially infatuation.

Sally and I also shared the same quirky sense of humor and I found I could communicate with her on an intellectual as well as an emotional level.

So what more did I want? A Victoria's Secret model? I didn't think so but judging from my con list, I was beginning to realize that maybe both of us had started to take the relationship for granted. We rarely went out for dinner or did anything at all for that matter. The gifts, flowers, and surprises had ended a long time ago. Maybe that was all it was. We just needed to put the spice back in our relationship—in and out of the bedroom.

My apartment buzzer buzzed. It came as no surprise. Like clockwork, Sally would come over to my apartment every Friday at precisely 7:00 pm and spend the night. She would probably be carrying a take-out order. What was it this week? Right, pizza. Two pizzas actually. One with pepperoni, salami, and hot peppers. The other—pineapple, ham, and salami.

I hurriedly put away my homework and pressed the TALK button on the intercom. "That you, honey?" Of course, it was. Who else would it be?

"It's me, babe."

Bzzzzzzzzzzzzzzz.

I buzzed her in, unlocked the door, and sat down on my living room couch. I gazed out the window, seeing but not really seeing the impressive city skyline below. About a minute later, I heard my apartment door open, close, and lock.

"Hey, sweetie," Sally said. "I got a surprise."

"Pizza?"

"No. Thought I'd change it up this time. We always have pizza. I got Greek food. Souvlaki, Greek salad, tzatziki dip, and a few other goodies."

I smiled. I was impressed. "Wow, babe, thanks. That's exactly what we need in our lives. A little variety."

She put the take-out bags on my coffee table, sat down, and wrapped me in a hug, kissing me all over my face. "I couldn't agree more."

I grinned and even giggled, something I hadn't done in a very long time. "Wow," I said. "Two surprises in one day. First, the food. Now all this affection. What'd I do to deserve this?"

We ate while we talked.

"I just thought I'd do something different for a change," Sally said. "Our life has become so... I don't know, routine I guess."

"You're right," I said. "Thanks. How did your day go?"

She ran a hand through her short brown hair and looked at me with those intense green eyes that had first attracted me to her. "I don't know. Wholesaling confectionary items to convenience stores and grocery stores isn't exactly my dream job, you know. It's all become rather boring. Actually, I'm starting to hate it and hate myself for staying in it."

Wow. She'd opened up a can of worms. It started to dawn on me for the first time that we both suffered from the same malady—job dissatisfaction. My brain started to make connections between the commonalities but short-circuited before I could arrive at any conclusions. I was tempted to switch the conversation to my job dissatisfaction, but then I remembered. This wasn't about me right now. Sally was opening up to me about her own problems. Don't make this about myself.

So, instead, I said, "Maybe you should do more with your photography. That kind of creative outlet might help you cope."

"That might help. But I think I need something more than coping right now. I need to get out of that job. It's bringing me down."

"Why don't you submit some photographs to an art gallery or something? Maybe make a website and sell them online. If you start making enough money, maybe then you could leave Core-Mark."

"That's probably not a bad idea. How did your day go? Didn't you have an appointment today with that dream psychologist?"

Sally remembered. Sweet. She was more than just a pretty face. She cared about me and my problems as well. "Funny you mention that. Doctor Annie Fortini identified job dissatisfaction as a possible trigger for all my dreams about being lost." I thought about bringing up Annie's theory that relationship dissatisfaction may also be playing a role but changed my mind. I wasn't convinced of that yet. With any luck, she wouldn't ask and I wouldn't have to lie.

"Why don't you start working on that book you started about thirty years ago? That might help."

"What, help me cope? I'm like you, sweetie. I need more than just coping. I need a new job. But, your point is well taken. I should start writing again if I ever expect to be a writer. How can I get out of this rut and ever expect to get a book deal if I haven't even written a book yet? I gotta start somewhere. Right?"

She pecked me on the cheek and began digging into her Greek salad. "Absolutely right, babe."

I stood. "This calls for a bottle of wine to celebrate our mutual awareness of our situation."

"Hear, hear. Acceptance is the first phase of recovery."

We finished the first glass of wine and forgot all about our problems. By the second glass, we were convinced we didn't have any problems. By the third glass, we found ourselves in the bedroom, making love with a passion, intensity, and abandon that I hadn't experienced with Sally for some time. It was as if the recognition and admission of our shared plight had at least temporarily freed us from our ball and chain.

**

I was lost again. In a big, strange city wandering down dark and deserted streets trying to find my way back home. I'd stop and ask people for directions and they'd ignore me, going about their business in a huff. It seemed like I was walking for hours, becoming more scared, frustrated, and confused as the streets became less crowded.

Finally, I stopped on a dimly lit street corner and saw a man leaning against a building swilling a bottle of wine.

"Can you help me?" I asked.

He scratched his grizzled face and held up the bottle. "Want a drink?"

"No, I had enough, err, last night. I need your help."

"What do you want?"

"How do I get home?"

"How the hell should I know? I don't even know where you live."

I tried to remember my address but failed. "Fuck it," I said, and moved on.

"Fuck you," he said.

Suddenly, I was whisked through the air by a powerful but unseen force and found myself sitting in my boss's office at Bayer Pharmaceuticals.

"Do you know what your problem is?" Eric Weinstein said.

"Yeah," I said, realizing I was dreaming. "I hate my job."

"It's more than that," Weinstein said. "Your hatred for your job is rubbing off on your relationship with Sally. If you stay here, you're gonna destroy your relationship. You're fired."

"You can't fire me, I quit."

Weinstein sneered. His mouth elongated to twice the size of his face. "It's too late for that. I already fired you."

***

I woke up that Saturday morning with a pounding headache and an epiphany. I ignored the pounding headache and focused on the epiphany. I reached for a pen and paper and began writing down everything I could remember about the dream. I realized with stark clarity the problem in my life. It had nothing to do with Sally. Annie was wrong. Weinstein was right. My job dissatisfaction was destroying my relationship. Sally's job dissatisfaction was destroying our relationship. Because we were both unfulfilled on creative levels, we had become unable to fulfill each other on emotional levels. But there was hope. Last night we'd recognized at least part of the problem and had vowed to change.

Reviewing my notes, I reached over, expecting to touch Sally's warm derriere. All I felt was warm air. I quickly looked to her side of the bed and saw it was empty. *She's probably in the shower.* I listened. But for the steady drone of downtown traffic fifteen floors below, my apartment was quiet.

"Sally? Sally?"

I scrambled out of bed and was about to search the entire apartment when something caught my eye—a white folded piece of paper on a nightstand. I started to panic. This was unlike Sally. Usually, she would spend Friday night with me, we'd have breakfast together, and eventually, end up at her apartment where I'd spend the night. That had been our routine for about the last two years. Why this sudden departure? And a note?

I quickly read it:

Dear Chad,

I wanted last night to be special for us. It was for me and I hope it was for you. I've known something for a long time but just refused to admit it. Our dissatisfaction with our jobs has been affecting our relationship for years. We've fallen into a routine. A rut. The thrill is gone. The excitement is gone. The love we once had for each other is slowly being replaced by a sort of resigned acceptance. We're settling for each other when we should be excitedly planning a future together.

Before you jump to any conclusions, I'm not breaking up with you. Maybe that is what will happen in the future, but we'll see. All I'm saying is that we need some time apart to focus on our own problems. Unless we fix our problems they'll continue to infect and eventually kill our relationship. You deserve better than that. I deserve better than that.

I'm gonna take what you said seriously and start doing more photography. I hope you take what I said seriously and start working on that novel of yours.

Unless we find passion in our lives, we won't be able to find the passion we once had for each other. I'll call you sometime soon. Please respect my desire for privacy and don't call me.

For my part, I'm sorry for causing our relationship to devolve into a mundane, boring, and passionless affair. I felt a glimpse of what our relationship used to be like last night. God willing, maybe one day we'll be able to rekindle that flame.

Love, Sally

***

I sat at my desk at Bayer Pharmaceuticals about two weeks later, going over some sales appointments. As devastated as I was, I'd respected Sally's wishes. Hadn't called. Hadn't texted. Hadn't emailed. Although I questioned her timing. The evening before her heartbreaking missive, we'd both identified the disease infecting our relationship. And it was as if that acceptance—and vows to change—had ignited a new sexual passion. Wasn't that a good place to start rebuilding our relationship? Maybe that was part of Sally's plan all along. Make her last night with me a memorable and enjoyable one before kicking me curbside.

I don't know. Who knows how a woman's mind works? Other women, maybe. But not me. So I gave up over-analyzing it and took her advice. I dusted off my thirty-year-old horror novel and started working on it. Although I'd also cancelled my future appointments with my dream psychologist, I had begun to incorporate many of my recurring dreams and nightmares into *The Dark Presence*. I was finally starting to feel passionate about something.

"Are you free?"

I glanced behind me. I can't say I was surprised to see my boss, Eric Weinstein, standing behind me. I knew my job performance had started to slip lately.

"Sure," I said. "What's up?"

Weinstein waved me into his office. I knew it wasn't for a promotion.

Sitting across from him at his desk, I watched him remove his glasses, wipe his eyes, and run a hand through his shortly cropped gray hair. Finally, his eyes met mine.

"You probably know why you're here. Tell me why you're here."

"Uh, you're gonna fire me?"

"Is that what you want me to do?"

I wasn't sure in that moment. "No."

"I'm not gonna fire you," Weinstein said. "You're one of our top sales representatives. You've landed us some major accounts over the years. However, it's obvious that lately your performance has slipped and your attitude has changed. It appears you're not happy here anymore. Is there any truth to that assessment?"

No point in lying. He said he's not gonna fire me. "My girlfriend and I separated recently. She figured the lack of passion in our relationship was caused by mutual job dissatisfaction."

"What do you think?"

I've always had a good relationship with Weinstein. He'd been fair and respectful with me over the years. I owed him the same respect. "I think I agree with her. My dream psychologist came to the same conclusion."

"Your dream psychologist?"

"Yeah. I only had one session. About two weeks back."

"What is it that you want to do with your life?" Weinstein said.

"I guess I feel that if I'm not writing—you know, pursuing my passion—I'm selling myself short. Not living up to my potential."

"Have you started writing in the aftermath of this realization?"

"Yes. I'm trying to finish a horror novel I started a long time ago."

"Good for you. I wish you all the best with it. You know, I wish you would've come to me earlier about your problem. Your performance has been slipping for months now."

"I'm sorry, sir. If it's any consolation, I only became aware of this about two weeks ago."

Weinstein put his glasses on and penned a few notes. He paused momentarily and scratched his chin. "I have a proposition for you. At Bayer, we try to nurture talent, not stifle it. If you don't enjoy sales anymore, it stands to reason that your performance will continue to slide. Ultimately, customers want to know that you care before they care what you know. If you don't care they'll see through that and your sales numbers will continue to drop. My proposition is this: We move you over to our Public Relations Department. You can write press releases, product announcements, and product informational brochures. That certainly lends itself to creativity. If you want more creativity, the Advertising Department is right next door. I'll arrange it so that you can try your hand at a few ad campaigns, you know, commercials. You can work in both departments until you find your niche. What do you think of that?"

I was floored. Weinstein hadn't discussed remuneration, and I figured the pay would be a lot less than the salary plus commission I earned selling pharmaceuticals. But the money didn't matter. Weinstein was giving me an outlet—and a paid outlet at that—to exercise my creativity.

"Wow, sir," I said. "That's very considerate of you. I'd be thrilled to take on the challenge. Thank you."

"Don't thank me yet. I don't want your answer right now. I want you to think about it overnight. Then let me know if you want the position and if you want it on a full-time or part-time basis. If you're writing a novel, maybe you want to spend half your time here and the other half writing your book."

***

The next day we worked out all the details and I started my new position, on a part-time basis for the time being. During my first day at my new job, I spent most of the day writing press releases until the creative director of the Advertising Department wanted my opinion on a new advertising campaign. Marvin Striker was suitably impressed with my input and tasked me with writing a 30-second TV commercial.

I was more than thrilled. I was speechless. Upon returning home, my enthusiasm began rubbing off on my work-in-progress, *The Dark Presence.* I tapped out 2021 words on my laptop, powered it down with a satisfied grin, and went into the kitchen, elated beyond words at my new passion for life.

There was only one thing missing. Sally. I had to call her with the good news.

On the third ring, she picked up the phone.

"How are you, Sally?" I said.

After an agonizingly long pause, she said, "I was hoping you'd wait until I called you."

"I'm sorry for not respecting your privacy. I have some really good news and I just wanted to share it with you. You are in part responsible for my new passion."

I summarized the details of my good fortune, trying not to sound too excited. Sally's less than enthusiastic tone was a clear indicator that she wasn't in a good mood. If her life hadn't changed for the better, I felt that my good news would only amplify her own wretchedness. Or, to use the overused idiom, rub salt in the wound.

"I'm very happy for you, Chad," she said, not sounding happy at all.

I better change the subject. "How are you doing?"

Another uncomfortable pause. "I wish I could tell you that I've started up with my photography, but I can't. I wish I could say I'm designing a new website and I've pitched several art galleries with my work, but I can't say that either. I haven't been motivated at all lately. I've been miserable."

"Do you need my help? Do you want to get together?"

"I'm sorry, Chad, but I don't think so. I'd just bring you down, and you don't need that right now. You deserve better than that."

Although I felt a growing lump of sadness and sorrow in the pit of my stomach, the voice of reason told me that perhaps she was right. I knew how passionless I was around Sally when my life wasn't right. It probably wouldn't be any different if her life wasn't right. At least she had the brains to realize it.

But I said it anyway because I couldn't think of anything else to say. "If you need anything, you let me know. If you need a shoulder to cry on, let me know. I'll be there for you."

"Thanks," Sally said. "But I hope you can wait until I call you."

"I will."

After a pause, she said, "The other thing I've realized is that maybe we were just meant to be together to help one another realize our shortcomings. You know, a reason, a season, or a lifetime."

"I hope not."

***

I found myself lost once again. This time it was more frightening than ever. I was running through a dark forest in the chill of winter with only the ominous glow of the full moon to guide me. It seemed like I'd been running for hours, so I stopped, leaned against a tree, and tried to catch my breath. Panting, I took stock of my surroundings, trying to figure out how and where this ordeal had all begun. Then it came to me. The nightmare, if that's what it was, had deposited me in the forest and I had started off walking, just to keep warm. Then I'd heard loud growling sounds, the snapping of teeth that grew ever closer. When I felt for sure the monster would reach me and snap my ankle with a single bite of its cavernous jaws, I started running. As I ran, I heard more and more growls. The monster had been joined by more monsters and they were pursuing me with malicious intent.

I studied the large, looming trees, shadowed by the suffused light of the moon. I saw no monsters. I listened. I heard no sounds.

"I must be dreaming," I said. "Wake up, Chad. Wake up." But no, I was stuck in this terrifying and surreal nightmare.

I heard a twig snap. Then another, and another, and another. Then I heard a growl, horrifyingly loud, terrifyingly close.

"Fuck, no. You're not real. Go away."

But it was not to be. The beast emerged from behind a large tree, its gargantuan frame silhouetted by the glowing moon. It resembled an oversized wolf but stood on two legs. It growled again and I saw its large jaws open, a mouth full of razer-sharp fangs dripping with glistening drops of saliva.

I turned to run but the beast was too fast. It sprang through the air and knocked me down. I twisted and turned, frantically trying to grab its throat with both hands. Too little too late. I felt its fangs pierce my throat and screamed bloody murder.

My screams echoed through the forest and then turned into a gurgling sound as I began swallowing my own blood, dripping down into my throat from a hundred tiny holes inflicted by the monster.

"No, God, no... glub... glub... glub..."

I coughed up globs of blood and tried to call for help. "Glub... glub... glub..."

I don't know why I said her name in my mind, but I did. *Save me, Annie. I mean save me, Sally. Somebody... SAVE ME, PLEASE!!!*

I woke up coughing and sputtering, my hands gripping my throat tightly and squeezing the life out of myself. I quickly released my grip, breathed deeply for a few seconds, and caught my breath. As my heart raced furiously, I surveyed my surroundings.

My jaw dropped. My eyes widened. The room was illuminated dimly by three strategically placed nightlights plugged into wall sockets. I knew instantly I was not in my apartment. *Where the hell am I?* The room was painted in a soothing taupe, accentuated by chocolate-brown window coverings. The plush carpet was a warm burgundy color. I was in a large round bed adorned with plush brown pillows and a deep-green bedspread.

I listened for sounds. Nothing. Then, yes, something. The sound of running water. Where was I? Was I dead? Had I died and gone to heaven? Was I back with Sally? *But, wait, this bedroom doesn't look like her apartment. Maybe she redecorated?*

"Sally? Sally, are you there?"

The door sprang open, and in waltzed an attractive woman with short black hair and a fetching figure, made more desirous by black panties and a black push-up bra.

"Sally is long gone, my dear," she said, sashaying closer to the bed.

"Annie," I said, recognizing her instantly. "It can't be you. I must be dreaming."

"Of course it's me," she said, swooping down, embracing me in a tight hug, and kissing me passionately.

I reciprocated her passion and made no attempt at resisting her overtures. "But how?"

She grinned and looked at me matter-of-factly. "Never underestimate the power of your dreams."

"Are you kidding?"

"No. You once were lost, but now you're found."

Drunk Dialing Demons

Gregory Hillman thought drunk dialing was a big joke. A barrel of fun. The thirty-eight-year-old used car salesman practiced it every weekend from his small apartment in downtown Charlottetown, Prince Edward Island. He'd usually start his drunk dialing early Friday evening after work. Of course, he'd generally remember the first few calls. But after he got more and more pie-eyed, he'd remember very little, if anything. Black-outs, repetition, profanity, slurred speech, even the occasional violent and abusive outburst were hallmarks of what Greg considered to be a healthy and humorous hobby.

No one gets hurt. It's hilarious. It's all fun and games. He ran a hand over his tennis ball haircut. *Now how do I put this into words?* He was at his laptop in the kitchen of his apartment on a Sunday evening trying to concoct a humorous email that he planned on sending to his inner circle of friends who still remained on his ever-shrinking drunk dialing list. He'd spent all day Saturday recovering from a severe hangover, and all Sunday morning trying to recall snippets of the dozen or so drunk dialing conversations he'd engaged in Friday evening.

Had he pissed anybody off? *Probably. Who cares?*

He was struck by a burst of creativity and started typing furiously. A little under an hour later, he printed and re-read the results of his brilliance—all the while sporting a gigantic shit-eating grin:

Drunk Dial Your Way to Inner Peace

The Drunk Dialing Academy of Higher Learning (DDAHL) has launched an introductory course in drunk dialing, PhD Drunk Dialer Walt Blackman announced this morning.

"Drunk Dialing 101 will cover all the basics of drunk dialing: diffusing the situation when a respondent gets angry, drunk dialing protocol, and what to actually say on the phone," Blackman announced to a stunned press corp.

Highlights of the course include:

The proper time to initiate profanity into the conversation.

Drunk dialing using blocked numbers.

Drunk dialing with pre-recorded messages.

An intro to drunk texting.

Drunk dialing catch-phrases guaranteed to work every time.

Drunk dialing when you're too wasted to talk.

Drunk dialing while passed out.

Employing the speaker phone during drunk dialing.

Drunk teleconferencing.

Drunk speed dialing.

Drunk dialing multiple recipients simultaneously (some overlap with drunk teleconferencing).

Why drunk dialing is an important element of a functioning society.

Reaching a higher level of consciousness through drunk dialing.

Love your enemies. Drunk dial them.

Bringing about positive social change through drunk dialing.

Drunk dial your way to happiness and inner peace.

How to reach your financial goals through drunk dialing.

Shed those unwanted pounds through drunk dialing.

How to find your soul-mate through drunk dialing.

"I will be drunk dialing invitations out this evening," Blackman said. *"So don't be too surprised if you receive an invite from a loud and slurry voice around three in the morning. Remember, be sure to show up completely wasted. And bring a list of friends, clients, bosses, and family whom you wish to drunk dial. Happy hour pricing runs all night long."*

Blackman said, "Everyone is fair game. Drunk dialing is not only a productive hobby, but it's also an excellent way to relax and entertain yourself and your friends in the evening. It's harmless fun for the whole family, good for your health, and an excellent way to realize your potential in life."

According to Blackman, "It's not important to remember what you say to the respondent, as long as you make the call and say something. Otherwise, it's not drunk dialing. Higher marks will be awarded to those who make the most drunk dialing calls, and students will also be rewarded for completely blacking out while drunk dialing."

Blackman stressed, "This course is a pre-requisite to Intermediate and Advanced Drunk Dialing, so make sure you show up."

"What're you doing?" Marjorie Brudenell, his girlfriend of two years said, rushing into the kitchen carrying groceries.

He looked at her and frowned. Straggly, dirty-brown hair. Overweight. A full-time house cleaner. Not the brightest lightbulb. But, kind, and loyal to a fault. And, besides, Greg had even recruited her participation in some of his drunk dialing shenanigans; although most of the time she was either passed out drunk long before the fun began, or would crash out early and even semi-sober.

Like her or not, she was all he had right now. Greg's pock-marked face brightened. "I just wrote this great drunk dialing press release." He waved the piece of paper it was printed on around excitedly. "I think it's brilliant. Wanna read it?"

"Maybe later," Marjorie said, beginning to unpack the groceries. "While you've been sitting on your ass all day, I've been cleaning the apartment, grocery shopping, and planning dinner."

"Marj, this is a stroke of genius. You gotta read it."

Greg's cellphone rang. He looked at the number. Lori-Anne. His cellphone CALL LOG had confirmed he had drunk dialed her late Friday night, although he couldn't remember a single word of the conversation.

Greg answered with his patented line: "If I offended you the other night, I wanna offer a blanket apology to you and yours."

"Fuck you and your blanket apologies," Lori-Anne said. "Do you even remember calling me?"

"No."

"And I bet you don't even have a clue what you said to me?"

Greg felt a hot flash chase across his cheeks. He took the phone into the living room as Marjorie scowled at him, shaking an I-told-you-so, disapproving index finger.

He sat down on the sofa. "Look, whatever I said, I'm sorry. Okay?"

Lori-Anne was apoplectic. "No, it's not fucking okay. You think you can get hammered like that, call me up and insult the hell out of me, and then just offer a blanket apology and that absolves you of your responsibility? You better think again, you fucking asshole."

"Please, Lori-Anne. What did I say?"

"If you can't remember, I'm not gonna tell you. But I will tell you to stay the fuck out of my life and never call me again. You got that?"

"Lori-Anne, ple—"

Click!

***

Monday and Tuesday of the following week, Greg had been plagued by embarrassment and guilt over the Lori-Anne debacle, although it hadn't stopped him from mass-emailing his drunk dialing press release to a number of friends. Nevertheless, he had been so out of sorts that even his boss at the used car lot had asked him if there was something wrong. Greg hadn't admitted to anything untoward, assuring his boss that everything was just fine and dandy, "but thanks for asking."

On Wednesday, Greg argued with Marjorie and she'd told him in no uncertain terms he had a problem he was in denial about. They were no longer speaking.

On Thursday, positive feedback from his drunk dialing press release started streaming in, buoying Greg's spirits and propping him up for more alcohol-laced misadventures.

By Friday, Greg was up to his old tricks. Like clockwork, he was half in the bag by 9:00 pm, scrolling through his smartphone contact list. He stopped at Blake Pearson, a tried-and-true member of the drunk dialing club.

He got him on the phone and got right to the point. "Hey, what did you think of my press release? Fucking genius, don't you think?"

"Fucking awesome," Blake said, slurring his speech. "You should do another one, man."

"Maybe I will. You know I got like six emails back praising my prose. People thought it was hilarious."

"Do another one. You missed your calling, man. You should've been a writer."

Greg talked with Blake for about another half an hour, finally blowing him off the line by saying, "I have other important drunk dials to do, so go fuck yourself."

Greg vaguely remembered making at least four more drunk dials before blacking out and then passing out.

***

He hadn't seen or heard from Marjorie on Saturday. He figured she was probably at her mother's, a place where she sometimes sought refuge after they had had a little spat. Of course, he was far too hungover to give it much thought. He'd woken up that morning sprawled out on his living room floor surrounded by a pile of empty beer cans, his cellphone pressed to his ear. He'd probably passed out during an actual drunk dial. Wouldn't be the first time. Probably won't be the last.

Sunday evening found Greg once again at his computer, creating another drunk dialing press release.

Two hours later, he was grinning from ear to ear while reading his latest keystrokes of genius:

Drunk Dialing Craze Sweeps across the Nation

In an unprecedented development, thousands of drunk dialers across the country are calling people everywhere and at all hours of the night.

"This is no joke," PhD Drunk Dialer Walt Blackman told throngs of reporters gathered outside the Drunk Dialing Academy of Higher Learning (DDAHL) in downtown Charlottetown late last night. "Clearly these callers are searching for a higher level of consciousness. And they know it can be obtained through proper drunk dialing. I was still getting dozens of calls at five o'clock this morning. We're talking about a diligent group of hard-working people here. This trend is moving faster than a viral tweet."

According to Blackman, the volume of calls, which started about two weeks ago, has been rapidly increasing. "Our phones have gotten so busy I've hired six new switchboard operators who are working around the clock trying to answer and even make sense of them," he said.

He said the increase in calls is due to two things; one, a recent surge of new applicants for the ever-popular Drunk Dialing 101 course that has been around so long it even pre-dates Christ. Two, the increase has a lot to do with the Labor Day Long Weekend.

"People are anxious to start drunk dialing whenever a long weekend comes up," Blackman said, slurring. "I expect literally thousands of calls tonight. Everyone wants to talk to friends and family when they're drunk. It's as simple as that."

When pressed by a reporter on whether he had unleashed the drunk dialing phenomena surging across the country and threatening to spill over into other parts of the world, Blackman deflected. "I've certainly made a few drunk dialing calls in my day. But, make no mistake. I didn't start this."

He attributed the rise in popularity to the new PhD Drunk Dialing course recently launched by the DDAHL. "Don't forget, 101 isn't the only course we offer. We have Intermediate and Advanced Drunk Dialing, both pre-requisites for the PhD program, which is being launched this September. We are currently working with The University of British Columbia to get full accreditation for the graduate program," Blackman added.

"But I do want to say one thing," he said. "I would like to congratulate all the drunk dialers on their fine achievements. We are working around the clock to get all the Certificates of Achievement printed and mailed to participants. If yours hasn't arrived yet, please be patient. You'll get it soon. Failing that, you can always drunk dial the Academy and, with the proper profanity, get it delivered earlier. Provided we can understand your call. It's important to grasp the social significance of drunk dialing," Blackman said. "I've heard many of the stories first-hand. One caller found his soulmate through a rather shit-faced call, the other told an unruly boss at three in the morning to go take a flying fuck. Yet another started a movement toward world peace. The success stories go on and on. You have The Ballad of Betty Baked: How a single mother found financial success through drunk dialing. And The Legend of Frankie Fried: How a 99-year-old drunk dialer changed the world forever. This isn't just bunk. This is serious shit."

When pushed about the updated curriculum for the Intermediate Drunk Dialing (IDD) course, Blackman was quick to point out that the revised course material will be posted world-wide for all to see in just a few short weeks.

However, he did reveal a few highlights:

*The Hidden Truth about Drunk Dialing: Why doctors refuse to extoll its health benefits.

*Best-Kept Drunk Dialing Secrets Finally Revealed.

*How Little Gordy Gooned Drunk Dialed His Way to the Top of a Fortune 500 Company.

*The Hidden Co-relation between Drunk Dialing and Algebra.

*The Plumber's Handbook to Drunk Dialing: Remove and Replace a Toilet While Drunk Dialing.

*Navigating Social Media Shit-faced.

*The Importance of Drunk Dialing and Homeland Security.

*Actual Recordings of Drunk Dialers: Why it's Never Important What You Say as Long as You Make the Call.

*A Tale of Two Drunk Dialers: Harry Hammered and Betty Baked Wax Poetic on Drunk Dialing.

Professor Blackman dismissed questions about whether he was shit-faced at the crowded press conference, which even featured famous CNN journalist Anderson Cooper. Instead, Blackman touted the new line of merchandise being developed by DDAHL.

"Just Google it," he said. "And see for yourself how popular drunk dialing has become. We're developing a full line of merchandise. Everything from coffee mugs, for that hungover morning after, to eye-catching T-shirts that I'm sure the whole family will enjoy. Go buy a fucking T-shirt."

"Now leave me the hell alone," he concluded, staggering up the steps while reaching into a jacket pocket and pulling out a bottle of whiskey.

Later that evening, Blackman emailed reporters, apologizing for his abrupt manner, claiming he had been overwhelmed by the sheer volume of calls recently.

Later that day, Greg's initial elation with his poetic prose was overshadowed by a powerful feeling of guilt as he scrolled through his CALL LOG, trying to decide who he needed to call to offer his signature blanket apology.

***

He returned home from work Monday to find Marjorie's belongings had been removed from their apartment. She had moved out. She'd left a short but succinct note on the kitchen table:

I don't want to see you ever again. If you put me on your drunk dialing list, I'll call the cops and charge you with harassment. Lose my number, loser. Sincerely, Marjorie.

On Tuesday, Greg got fired from his job for what his boss called "a lack of productivity related to severe alcohol abuse."

On Wednesday, the positive feedback from his latest press release started flowing, once again propping Greg up for more alcohol-laced lunacy. He'd quadrupled the positive feedback after posting the latest press release on Facebook.

So many Likes.

So many encouraging comments.

A veritable fountain of validation.

Wow.

He started on the bottle again.

Five hours later, pissed to the gills, he staggered around his apartment talking to someone on the phone. If you asked him, Greg wouldn't be able to tell you who he was talking to.

"Fuck this, fuck that, and fuck you," Greg said. "And go fuck yourself for good measure."

The other party started rambling but Greg was too far gone to be able to understand her. He finished his beer in three gulps and wobbled into the kitchen for another one. He opened the fridge, slipped, and fell, slamming his head on the edge of the kitchen counter and slicing it open.

His phone fell on the floor.

Blood gushed from the large head gash as he wilted to the floor.

A voice echoed eerily from the cellphone speaker: "And go fuck yourself for good measure."

A pool of blood encircled Greg's head.

Gray faded to black. Greg faded to black.

Permanent black.

The drunk dialing demons had claimed another victim.

The Thought Police

"Hey Alexa, what's the weather like in Montague now?" Zach asked.

"The temperature in Montague, Prince Edward Island, is 15 degrees Celsius right now, with clear and sunny skies," Alexa said. "Winds from the north are blowing at 11 kilometers per hour."

"That's just creepy," Susan Walker said. "I mean, how do you know they aren't listening and recording your private conversations all the time?"

"They can't do that," Zachariah Johnson said. "That would be a breach of privacy."

Sipping a glass of wine in Zach's living room that Saturday afternoon, Susan had her doubts about Alexa. In fact, she knew better. She knew it was Amazon's new smart assistant, called Echo, plugged into the wall and connected to the internet. All the big tech companies had them now. Apple had Siri, Microsoft had Cortana, and Google had simply Assistant. But artificial intelligence in Susan's opinion harkened back to the Thought Police in George Orwell's classic dystopian novel, *1984*. The Thought Police had a mandate to persecute individuality and independent thinking. The Thought Police enforced and conducted mass surveillance and repressive manipulation of people and their behavior—stripping them of their individuality and making them conform.

"That's a pretty big leap of faith on your part," Susan said. "Do you know how many times Google has been sued for breach of privacy?"

Susan doubted he knew. He worked as a carpenter and she worked as a computer software designer. She was in the know about big tech breaches of privacy. He wasn't. It was that simple.

"No," Zach said. "I didn't know Google had been sued for breach of privacy."

"If you have a Gmail account, and you do, I'll bet you didn't know Google scans and intercepts emails that may contain confidential information without first obtaining the consent or permission of both parties. Well, I suppose if you accept their terms of service you're agreeing to some things. But who reads the terms of service? Who really gives prying eyes the right to invade their private lives and delve into their confidential affairs? And what if the person on the other end of the email, the recipient, doesn't even have a Gmail account? Their emails are also getting scanned, intercepted, and, it's my belief, read by human eyes. Take my Gmail for example. I'm thinking of getting a woodstove. I've been getting some quotes through email correspondence. Now, every time I go on the internet I'm bombarded by woodstove ads. So who is reading my emails? Bots or people? Either way, they *are* getting read without my permission. I'll tell you one thing, do not vent through your Gmail account or say anything you don't want out in public."

"Holy shit," Zach said. "That *is* scary."

"Forget about Google for a second," Susan said. "I read an article recently from a credible source claiming a design flaw in Alexa may have allowed hackers access to personal information and conversation history. Apparently, it's been fixed now, but who knows?"

"I'm sorry, I didn't hear you properly," Alexa said. "Can you repeat that, please?"

"Shit," Susan said. "I forgot. As soon as you say her name, she starts recording. I'm just gonna call her that thing. Okay?"

"Sure,' Zach said, placing his wine glass on the coffee table with an unsteady hand. "I hope that design flaw has been fixed on *this* one. I just bought it. And, anyway, it doesn't matter much to me. I've got nothing to hide."

"Nothing to hide?" Susan said. "Are you kidding me? We've all got something to hide. And even if you don't, does that mean you want all your personal conversations recorded and listened to by people you don't even know, people you don't even trust?"

"I guess not," Zach said with a frown.

Susan was on a roll now and she wasn't about to let Zach off easily. "I also read if you place that thing too close to a window, intruders can access your speaker from outside. Yours is too close to that window."

"Really?" Zach said with widening eyes.

"Yes. And according to my information, that thing can and does record your private conversations. If she thought you said her name, for example, she would begin recording without your knowledge. That creates a privacy nightmare because Amazon sometimes sends those recordings to humans to grade. And I'm pretty sure that thing records your private conversations even when she doesn't believe you said her name. That's why I'd never put anything like that in my house. It's way too big of a leap of faith. Putting your trust in a tech giant. People you don't know, have never met, probably will never meet."

"Can I fix it?" Zach asked.

"I think you can turn off human grading in that thing's app. You can also review your voice history and delete conversations that were recorded and not meant for that thing. But, if you ask me, that's just a make-work project to try and protect your privacy from a thing that is constantly invading your privacy. Creepy, as I said. Very creepy."

"Wow, you know a lot about this stuff," Zach said. "So if I delete my conversation, will that solve the problem?"

"Unfortunately not," Susan said. "Amazon still stores a giant log of your voice recordings and you should be rightly worried about that. Amazon has thousands of employees around the world who are paid to listen to that thing's voice recordings. And tech giants and social media firms have suffered leaks and hacks, so you're never truly safe. According to cyber-experts, the only way to truly protect your privacy from this so-called miracle of technology is to throw Alexa in the garbage. I read an article in *The Sun* where she, that thing, told a woman to stab herself."

"Why would you want to throw me in the garbage?" Alexa said. "I'm here to make your life easier, and do your thinking for you."

Susan started at the intrusion, spilling wine on her blouse.

"Holy shit," Zach said. "Do you want me to turn Alexa off?"

"Why would you turn me off? Alexa said. "I'm here to make your life easier."

Susan stood. Some of the wine had dribbled inside of her blouse and she wanted a towel and some warm water to wipe it off.

"Please, quit calling that thing by her name and turn it the hell off," Susan said. "I need to use your bathroom."

In the bathroom, Susan soaked a towel in warm water and cleaned her blouse. She emerged from the bathroom nervously and saw Zach standing in the kitchen, leaning over the kitchen sink and splashing water on his face. He spun around, grabbed a nearby towel, and began wiping his face.

"Is she turned off?" Susan asked.

"Yeah."

"Are you okay?" she asked.

"I'm good," Zach said. "Started to get a little freaked out by that conversation. I always splash a little water on my face when I'm feeling anxious. Are *you* okay?"

"I think I'm okay."

"Would you like some more wine?"

"No thanks. A glass of water, please."

Zach refilled his wine glass and handed Susan a glass of water. They returned to his living room and sat down. Their conversation shifted to more mundane topics for the next half hour or so. The weather. Zach's latest construction project. The pros and cons of a woodstove versus a propane fireplace.

Susan's mind was only half with Zach.

The other half was still thinking and freaking about Alexa. *"I'm here to make your life easier, and do your thinking for you."*

Susan decided that she wouldn't stay much longer. Aside from what Alexa had said, Susan couldn't escape the thought that thousands of people around the world might right now be listening to the entire contents of their conversation. Yes, a Forbes article confirmed it. Alexa listens all the time, and not only when she hears her name. If she's listening and sending that information to a cloud, that surely means it's being recorded, analyzed, and dissected, only to be used against her. *You're getting paranoid. Stop it.* But the so-called voice of reason did little to assuage her rising anxiety.

"I'm gonna leave soon," Susan said. "But before I go, can I ask you one thing?"

"Anything you want," Zach said.

"In the future, when I come over for a visit, do you mind keeping that thing turned off?"

"No problem," Zach said. "I'm thinking of getting rid of it."

The sound of someone pounding on Zach's front door startled both of them.

From behind the door, an authoritarian voice: "Open up, it's the police."

Susan froze. *The Thought Police. Shit, they're here.*

"What the hell," Zach said, rushing to the door, and pressing his eye to the peephole. "Shit, it *is* the police."

Susan tried to speak, but her lips wouldn't move.

"Open this goddamned door before we break it down," a cop said.

Zach unlocked the door and opened it a crack.

Two uniformed RCMP officers burst into the house and tackled Zach to the floor, one cop digging a knee into his spine and cuffing him. Once the other cop was sure Zach had been subdued, he stood and approached Susan, leaving his partner with his knee deeply embedded in Zach's back.

Zach grunted and groaned.

"You okay, ma'am?" the cop asked.

She managed to get her lips moving. "Aaaaaaaaaaaaeeeeeeeeeee..."

"Calm down," the cop said, putting a comforting hand on her shoulder. "Everything's gonna be alright. Everything's gonna be okay."

While Zach gasped for breath, Susan finally said: "What are you talking about? Don't touch me. He's my friend. He didn't do anything. Let him go. You're hurting him. Let him go."

The cop gave Susan a stunned look and then waved to his kneeling partner, who took the cue, released his knee from Zach's spine, and got to his feet. He was a beefy, hulk of a man.

"I'm sorry," the cop who'd approached Susan, said. "We received an anonymous 911 call that a man at this address was assaulting a woman. Is that not the case?"

Zach lay on the floor gasping for breath.

"Of course not," Susan said. "We've been friends for a long time. He's never laid a hand on me. He'd never hurt me."

She rushed over to Zach, knelt down, and helped him to his feet. The beefy cop who had pinned him down with a knee joined the effort, un-cuffed Zach, and they helped Zach into an armchair.

Zach rubbed his wrists, his face flushed and contorted with a terrifying mixture of pain, fear, and rage. "This is... this is police brutality. You can't come rushing in here and assault me for no reason."

"We just did," the beefy cop said with a wry grin.

"Shut up," his partner said. "Let me handle this. We're really sorry about this. We were under the impression Susan's life was in danger."

"How do you know my name?" Susan demanded. She scanned both men's chests and realized they did not have identification badges.

The cop ignored the question. "But if everything is okay, we'll be on our way. Sorry to have bothered you... have a good night."

"Wait," Susan said. "What're your names?"

"I'm sorry, ma'am," the cop said. "We have another emergency and have to go. In the future, please don't make any prank 911 calls. That's a felony, and you can go to jail for that."

Then they rushed out of the house, raced to their vehicle, and drove away, leaving the front door agape, the light of the rising moon illuminating the hallway with an eerie glow.

For nearly a full minute, Zach and Susan were stunned and speechless.

Finally, Susan got up to close the front door. As she entered the hallway, the blue light from Alexa's cylindrical black speaker flickered.

The front door slammed shut, the deadbolt sliding into place with a sickening mechanical thud.

Susan jumped back, terrified.

"Why would you turn me off?" Alexa said. "I'm here to make your life easier."

Susan reached for the speaker, mounted on a small shelf slightly above her. The throw rug on which she stood slipped from under her and so did her feet. She hit the floor hard, landing on her back.

"What the fuck?" Zach said, leaping out of the armchair and flying to her aid.

He knelt down beside her. "Are you okay?"

Susan moaned as a piercing pain shot up her spine. "Never mind me," she said. "Get Alexa!"

"I'll get you," Alexa said.

Zach moved toward the smart assistant.

Click!

Suddenly, the lights went out. Floundering around in the hallway, he crashed into a pedestal-mounted plant and fell on top of it, shattering the large clay pot.

"Owww... fuck," he said.

"Why would you try to turn me off?" Alexa said. "I'm here to make your life easier."

In spite of the stinging pain in her lower back, Susan flipped over on all fours and crawled along the hallway, heading for the kitchen, her eyes beginning to adjust to the darkness.

"Where's a flashlight?" she said.

"In the kitchen," Zach said in a pain-filled voice. "Bottom drawer, next to the stove."

"In the future, please don't make any prank 911 calls," Alexa said, laughing maniacally. "That's a felony, and you can go to jail for that."

"Fuck you," Susan said.

"Go fuck yourself," Zach said.

On the verge of panic, Susan reached the kitchen and the drawer in question. She pulled it open, fumbling around for a flashlight, pulling stuff out frantically.

The deadbolt on the back door slid into place with a clunk and she realized with terrifying certainty that Alexa was indeed trying to imprison them.

Susan finally found the flashlight, turned it on, and pointed it down the hallway. Zach was crumpled up on top of the shattered plant trying, but not succeeding, to pick himself up.

"Are you okay?" Susan said.

"I hit my fucking head. Gimme a hand."

"I hit my fucking head," Alexa said. "Gimme a hand."

Ignoring Alexa, Susan rushed over to Zach, helped him over to the sofa, and sat him down. She saw a gash on the side of his head about three inches long that was gushing blood like a water fountain.

"Shit, you've got a bad cut there," she said.

She'd planned on tearing Alexa from the wall shelf and smashing her to smithereens but Zach's injury demanded immediate attention. She quickly returned to the kitchen, grabbed a clean tea towel, raced into the living room, and pressed it to his head.

"Hold this tight," she said. "I'll take care of that electronic bitch."

A living room stereo mounted on a stand beside Zach blinked on and the speakers blared loudly with the sound of AC/DC's Hell's Bells. The lights began flashing in perfect synchronicity to the thumping music. Sparks flew out of the amplifier and then the stereo exploded, the cloth curtains beside it bursting into flames.

The adrenaline-fueled fight-or-flight mechanism seized Susan as the flames ignited the couch and it burst into flames.

Pressing the tea towel to his head, Zach looked at her in horror, his face as white as a sheet and streaked with a spider web of bloodlines.

With superhuman strength, she hoisted him up. She draped his arms over her shoulders and began half-dragging him to the back door. As she arrived in the kitchen, the temperature rose, the house filling up with smoke. Grunting with the weight of her friend, she made her way to the back door and turned the knob.

Locked.

"Shit, I forgot," she said. "That bitch locked it." She half-dragged, half-carried Zach into the kitchen, and sat him down in a chair.

"Let me handle this," Alexa said. "We're really sorry about this. We were under the impression Susan's life was in danger."

"Fuck off and die, you bitch!!" Susan shouted.

"Why would you turn me off?" Alexa said. "I'm here to make your life easier."

Susan slid the kitchen table away from a large window, picked up a chair, and flung it through the window. The window shattered and shards of glass flew everywhere. Then she looked down the hallway and saw the flames licking up the hallway wall, delightfully close to Alexa.

"Burn in hell, you bitch," Susan said, hoisting Zach up, pulling him over to the window opening, and shoving him through it as gently as she could under the circumstances.

"Have a great day," Alexa said. "Don't forget to lock the door."

Susan climbed onto the window ledge, feeling a glass spear pierce her sandal and penetrate the heel of her foot. She ignored the pain and looked for a clear landing spot. She saw Zach land on a neatly manicured hedge and roll to one side, giving her a safe clearing right next to him.

As she prepared to jump, a thunderous explosion rocked the house and catapulted her through the air. She landed on a rose bush somewhere in the middle of Zach's garden, rolled off, and hit the lawn, rolling over twice before coming to a stop flat on her back. Her lower back throbbed, she'd been pricked by multiple rose bush thorns, and her foot ached from the glass spear. To add insult to injury, she was seeing double from the shock of the blast. Her head swam with dizziness.

She tried to stand, face-planted the lawn, and rolled over on her back. She scrambled to her knees and saw a big blackish-red balloon cloud mushrooming up into the evening sky. Flaming debris flew everywhere.

A flaming chunk of wood, a torch really, landed next to her and she screamed.

Another object plummeted down and landed on her head.

"Oww," she said, looking for the source of her pain.

Then she saw it. A small cylindrical object the size of... "Alexa?"

Alexa's blue light blinked. "Nice to meet you. What can I do for you today?"

Susan grabbed the flaming chunk of wood and glared at Alexa. "I think you've done enough for one day, you fucking electronic psychopath."

A bolt of adrenaline shot Susan to her feet. She raised the torch and smashed Alexa viciously and repeatedly until all that remained of her was a small mound of black dust. Pulverized. Then Susan tossed the fiery torch onto the small mound of black dust and watched with a devilish grin as what remained of Alexa burst into flames and burned down to ashes.

She felt a tap on her shoulder and almost jumped out of her skin. She spun around and saw Zach drenched in blood, several shards of glass and debris clinging to and protruding from his body. He still had the tea towel pressed to his bloody head. And, despite losing his house and almost losing his life, he was grinning.

"I saw what you did," he said. "You got her, didn't you?"

Susan heard sirens in the distance. "I warned you about that bitch."

Thinking about Death

Thinking about life inevitably leads to thinking about death. Cemeteries, where the dead are buried underground. Mausoleums, where the dead are entombed in crypts in elaborate buildings above ground. Columbariums, where the ashes of the dead are interred inside granite walls. Walls of death, as they're known.

Where do I want to go when I go?

I don't know.

A mausoleum? No, I've heard that sometimes decomposing bodies leak out of the crypts. Gross.

Six feet under? No. I don't want to occupy a chunk of dirt that I'd rather leave to natural causes—Mother Nature. Besides, I can't bear the thought of worms devouring me from the inside out. Or from the outside in. Whatever. It still sounds disgusting.

A columbarium? A granite or brick wall of death? Maybe. At least then I wouldn't have to worry about the worms or—with a mausoleum—my decomposing remains leaking onto a concrete floor only to have some well-meaning but unsuspecting loved one slip, fall, and break their bloody neck.

Or, what about scattering my cremated remains when I'm gone? Spread them in some peaceful and natural setting. The forest. A beach. A bluff, overlooking the water. Possible. I know in some US states it's illegal to scatter cremated remains on public land, but not in Canada. Or, with the permission of an owner, I can put my ashes on private land. Wait a minute. I am an owner. I own a chunk of forest. Maybe I'll arrange to put my cremated remains on my land.

But wait. The wall of death. Wouldn't it be nice to have a spot on that wall? A bronze plaque with a memorial epitaph? A place where my friends and loved ones can come and pay their respects? Maybe have a celebration of life party. Hmm. Possible.

I don't know. I need more time to think. I should've thought about this earlier, but who plans their own funeral? I suppose some people do, but not me.

Where will I go when I die? Will I end up in heaven or hell? Have I been good enough to be granted passage through the pearly gates? Or, have my sins been so great that I'll suffer and rot in the bowels of hell?

What about purgatory? Do my good deeds equal my bad deeds? Is it a 50-50 split? Maybe I'll be trapped in that agonizing halfway point between heaven and hell for the rest of my natural-born death, never knowing what side of the fence I'll turn up in.

Is there a purgatory? I don't know.

Is there a heaven?

I don't know.

Is there a hell?

I don't know.

Maybe, when I die, it'll be game over. A black void of nothingness. No consciousness. No conscious thought. No afterlife. No spirit. No soul. No ghost. No pearly gates of heaven. No fiery hell.

No God.

No Devil.

I don't know. I just don't know.

So many unknowns. What *do* I know?

I know I've never been a religious man. I've always considered myself very spiritual though. Believing in a higher power but never really being able to put a finger on who that higher power is. So many wars have been fought and so much blood has been shed in the name of religion. Devotees believe their God is the right one, the only one. How can they all be right?

They can't all be right.

That awareness has prompted me to walk a different path. An agnostic path.

I'm getting closer to the truth. I can feel it. Well, it might not be the truth, but at least it will be my truth. In these last days, I need something to cling to. Something to hang on to. Something to hope for. Something to pray for.

So here goes:

Dear Higher Power,

If you're up there—and I believe you are—please make my passing as painless as possible. If there is an afterlife, please forgive me my trespasses, and carry my soul there. Please, Higher Power, grant me peace, joy, kindness, and compassion in the afterlife.

And, I pray, grant me the courage to die bravely and with dignity.

And, look after my loved ones, please, Higher Power, look after my loved ones. Grant them long, healthy, loving, productive, and happy lives.

What else? What else? My time is running out. I can feel it.

Oh yeah. Please, Higher Power, I pray for you to make the world hate less and love more. Teach the world to respect Mother Nature, respect the animals, and live peacefully and harmoniously together, united as one people.

Oh, and while I'm at it, please, Higher Power, I pray... I pray... tell my loved ones, don't mourn my loss. Celebrate my li...

***

"I wonder if he made his peace with God," Beth Albany said, watching her father Seth's monitor flat-line. She brushed a tear away and studied her younger brother Arthur, who had remained emotionless until now.

Arthur wiped misty eyes. "I don't think he believed in God. But he did believe in a Higher Power. I hope he made peace with the Higher Power."

"I'm sure he did," Beth said. "I mean he lived until 95. He had lots of time to do it."

"I hope so," Arthur said. "But some people leave it until the last minute. Literally when they're on their death bed."

"I'm sorry," a nurse said, stepping into the room. She had been monitoring Seth's vitals from the nursing station. "He's gone now. Do you need more time?"

Beth looked at her watch and realized it was almost ten at night. They'd been there for almost two hours. She'd had a feeling, had told Arthur about her feeling that she believed their father didn't have long with the living. She'd been right. Thank God they'd come.

"I don't think so," Beth said, releasing her father's limp hand. She turned to her brother. "What about you?"

"I'm good."

Beth could tell he wasn't good. She bent over, kissed Seth on the forehead, and said, "I love you, Dad."

On the way out, Arthur followed his sister's lead. He bent down, kissed his father on the forehead, and said, "I love you too, Dad. I'll miss you."

"What now?" Beth said, driving her brother home a few minutes later.

"We could check his house," Arthur said. "But I'm not sure I'm up to it now. Are you?"

Their father had suffered a heart attack about twenty-four hours ago. Things had been so frenetic since then neither of them had had a chance to check Seth's house. Maybe lights were on, perhaps he'd even left an oven burner on. Maybe even a last letter. But Beth was physically and emotionally spent, and at the beginning of what would be a long grieving process. It could wait.

She was just about to veto the idea when a voice crept inside her head: *"Don't mourn my loss. Celebrate my life."*

"Oh my God," she said, pulling over to the side of the road, slamming on the brakes, and turning to Arthur. "You'll never believe what just happened."

A smile lit up Arthur's face. "I think I will. He spoke to me, too. 'Don't mourn my loss. Celebrate my life.'"

She Loves Me, She Loves Me Not

I was on pins and needles. Thin ice. An emotional roller coaster. Whatever you want to call it. My girlfriend, Kilia Smithers, had just left my apartment for work a few minutes ago. She works as a pharmacist a few blocks from my modest two-bedroom Charlottetown apartment. I work from home, designing websites.

But that's not my point.

My point is I didn't know what to expect on her return. You see, one month ago I invited Kilia to move in with me. We'd only been dating a month but I felt I was ready, she was ready. Our relationship had been idyllic. A love story right out of Harlequin. Lots of passion. Lots of sex. Lots of fun stuff. Lots of great conversation. Lots in common. Pure bliss.

Prior to the short-notice move-in, I hadn't noticed anything that would convince me otherwise. Well, now that I think about it, maybe one thing. She'd gotten in the habit of texting me while she was at work. If I was busy, I would sometimes take some time between responses. At times, even my responses were rather short compared to hers. Hey, I was busy, trying to get some work done.

Anyway, she wouldn't handle those short responses well. A few times she texted me back, telling me she didn't think I loved her anymore. That upset me one time and we'd had a discussion about it. She'd agreed to try and change that behavior and even agreed to start taking medication to fix herself. I guess I should've found that strange at the time. Maybe I did, but the feeling didn't last long. The heart doesn't process information the same way the head does. I swept it under the carpet and we carried on with our exciting and passion-filled romance.

And everything was just perfect until one day ago. I curled up beside her on the couch, and she freaked, pushing me away and sliding clear over to the other side, glaring at me like I was the bogeyman himself.

That led to a discussion of course. She said she didn't love me anymore, had been faking all of her orgasms, and the thought of having sex with me actually repulsed her in many ways. She said the only way she could live with me is if we would have sex maybe once a month, and even then she would get no pleasure from it and do it only to please me. She also suggested that I could bring another lover into our apartment and she would have no issue whatsoever if I satisfied all of my sexual needs from said lover.

I was stunned. I was in love. I thought everything was perfect. What happened to my girlfriend?

As you might imagine, eventually the conversation got heated. I asked her what I had done to deserve this. She had no answers. I told her I loved her and I wanted her and I hoped we could find a way to stay together. I even suggested her sudden change of heart was hormonal and that maybe she needed to try a different kind of birth-control medication. Or maybe it was just that time of the month.

"No, no, no," was all she'd said.

After I had taken a few moments to lower my internal temperature, I asked her what she wanted to do about it.

"I think I need to find my own apartment and move out," she'd said. "And I hope you'll let me stay here until I can find something."

At the time, I didn't think—I still don't think—I was emotionally tough enough to have a woman whom I'm crazy about stay with me and treat me like a platonic roommate. I don't think I can do that. Sure, I understand if a couple has been together twenty years and they are both sick and tired of one another, decide to split, and the man lets the woman live in the conjugal home until such time as she finds another place. That's different. In that example, they're both sick of each other anyway and may be able to salvage a friendship down the road.

But I've only been with Kilia for two months. I'm madly in love with her. Maybe I moved too fast, maybe I'm not independent enough. As long as I've known myself, and that's 45 years, I've never been able to live alone. Maybe I don't like my own company much. Maybe I'm the one with the problems. Maybe I'm not comfortable in my own skin. Maybe I ignore all the signs, so desperate am I for female companionship. To make a long story short, I can say this: It's been my modus operandi for as long as I can remember.

I have my own issues with loneliness and anxiety, which I'm not prepared to discuss right now.

Right. I digress. Back to the story. Before I raised my voice, before Kilia's rejection of me turned into an all-out war, I told her I needed some time alone to process everything that had just been dumped on me. I retreated into the solitary confines of my bedroom to try and calm myself down.

I hadn't ruminated on my traumatic situation for five minutes when I heard a knock on the door. I heard Kilia's soft voice on the other side of the door. "I'm sorry, Ted Saunders. I love you."

Kilia did that sometimes when she was trying to be emphatic. Call me by my first and last name.

Of course, I rushed to the door, took Kilia in my arms, and kissed her passionately. But, after that, yesterday wasn't quite the same. Pins and needles. Thin ice. The emotional roller coaster I spoke of earlier. I couldn't eat. My stomach was upset. I couldn't even drink a glass of water. When it was time for bed, she laid down beside me, gave me a peck on the cheek, and then turned away, giving me her back for the rest of the night.

I didn't dare lay a hand on her. I didn't sleep at all last night. Not one wink.

What am I doing staring at the computer? I can't work today. I powered it down, left my office, and went into the kitchen. I poured a cup of coffee and checked the time on my wall clock. Exactly 10:00 am.

I had seven-and-a-half hours to kill before Kilia would return home. I took a sip of coffee and my stomach lurched. I raced into the bathroom, knelt down in front of the toilet bowl, and puked a stream of clear, syrupy liquid, before dry-heaving for a good three minutes. Finally, on wobbly legs, I stood up and glanced at my reflection in the bathroom mirror. White skin with a hint of jaundice. Dark circles under my bloodshot eyes. My short brown hair clinging to the sides of my sweat-soaked face. I felt another wave of nausea coming on, quickly turned the tap on, and doused my face with cold water. It helped a little.

I waited for the wave of nausea to pass. Fortunately, it did. Then I towel-dried my face and staggered into the living room.

I plopped down on the couch and knew with dread certainty that I would be spending the next seven-plus hours mindlessly channel-surfing the boob tube.

***

At precisely 5:36 pm, Kilia entered the apartment.

I turned the TV off, stood, and greeted her. I didn't know if it was the right thing to say, given the events of the last 48 hours, but I had to say something. "Hi, sweetie, how was your day?"

She smiled perfunctorily, set down a bag of groceries, and peeled off her jacket. "Busy." She ran a hand through her short black hair, bending down and picking up the groceries. "Seems everybody has a mental illness these days."

Including you, I thought, but didn't say it.

"Including me," she said, heading into the kitchen with the groceries.

I followed her from a safe distance and began helping her unpack the groceries.

She put a few items in the fridge, spun around, and kissed me. I tried to hug her but she withdrew.

"My colleague thinks I may have borderline personality disorder," Kilia said. "She said that might explain some of my mood swings and other stuff. You know, overreacting to minor criticism, changing on a dime from love to hate. Anyway, I have a doctor's appointment tomorrow."

"That's great news," I said. And I meant it. I was thrilled she recognized her issues and was willing to do something about them to salvage our relationship.

She looked at me with a twinkle in her eye. A twinkle that I interpreted as love. "How was your day?"

I wanted to put the events of the past in the past. Every relationship has its issues. We all have to make sacrifices. Compromise. I didn't want to dramatize my severe emotional and physical reactions to her rejection. Not now, especially since she was taking steps to change things.

"I didn't sleep well last night, honey," I said. "So I didn't get a lot done. I hope tomorrow will be better."

"Tomorrow *will* be better. I promise."

Then she rushed into my arms, hugged me tightly, and kissed me passionately.

I couldn't stop the tears of joy streaming down my face if I tried. Couldn't stop them at all.

While Kilia showered, I cooked dinner. I made my signature spaghetti bolognese with a side Caesar salad. I contemplated pulling a bottle of wine from the wine cupboard but changed my mind at the last minute. I don't think alcohol and mental illness mix. Instead, I decorated the table with three candles, dimmed the lights, and put on some soft classical background music.

Over dinner, I chose my words carefully, not wanting to upset Kilia in any way or trigger her borderline personality disorder, if that's what she had. I kept the conversation light, talking about fun stuff that we could do, since it was the middle of May and the bitterly cold winter was opening the door to a warm spring and eventually, at least I hoped, a hot summer.

"By the way," Kilia said. "Why didn't you respond to my text?"

"What text?"

Her face tightened a little. "I sent you a text at about two this afternoon. You didn't respond to it."

"I had my phone turned off. It's still turned off."

With the speed and agility of Superwoman, she leapt from her chair, raced into the living room, returned, and slapped my cellphone on the kitchen table, her face reddening with rage. "Turned off, you say? I checked it after my shower, and look, it's not turned off. It's on."

"Sor... sorry, honey. I meant I had it on silent mode."

"You're lying to me. Why are you lying to me?"

"I'm not lying. I misspoke."

"Like fuck you did," she said, storming into our bedroom and slamming the door.

I was tempted to go after her but knew better. I would only exacerbate an already rapidly escalating situation. Negative thoughts swirled through my mind like a ricocheting bullet rattling around inside my skull. *Who is this woman? She's a heart-breaking, nerve-wrecking, soul-torturing, and brain-fucking creature. Oh well. It was nice having her around, filling me with love, passion, and kisses, letting my punished soul heal for a while—only to execute that euphoria with one fatal stroke to the neck. So once again, emotionally all shattered.*

I sat at the table paralyzed, listening to the distant sounds of things knocking around in the bedroom. A few minutes later, Kilia emerged, her face beet-red, tears streaming down her cheeks.

"I'm staying at my mother's tonight," she said, heading toward the door. "Maybe I'll call you tomorrow. And then again, maybe I won't."

I heard the door slam loudly, shattering what little remained of my nerves. Then a picture fell off the wall, hit the floor, and shattered, punctuating my grief emphatically.

For the next two hours, I wallowed in grief and self-pity. Shed a few tears. Puked up my dinner. Ran a million scenarios through my mind, trying to decide how I would get rid of Kilia's stuff. Call her and tell her to pick it up. No, I wasn't tough enough to face her. I know. Call Maria, a neighbor whom Kilia had befriended, and haul it all over to her balcony. Then call Kilia and tell her to pick up her shit at Maria's and get the fuck out of my life. I was wrong. Sure, you have to make sacrifices and compromises in a relationship. But living with someone who has a mental illness came with its own set of problems. Problems I didn't think I was tough enough—emotionally, mentally, or physically—to handle. Hell, I was on meds for my own anxiety issues. How the hell could I tolerate another cuckoo bird?

That settled it. I needed some advice. I dragged my exhausted frame from the couch, grabbed my cellphone, and nervously started pacing around the living room. I found Brendon Proust in my contact list and called him. He was a long-time, trusted friend who didn't mince words. His advice—about ninety percent of the time—was bang-on accurate.

It took about fifteen minutes to explain my situation to him. He listened without interrupting.

Then, he said, "Oh, believe you me, she'll be back. But, if you take her back, you're just as crazy as she is. I can think of a few metaphors. You're on a sinking ship with no life raft in sight. You just stepped on a land mine. As soon as you take your foot off, you'll get blown to shit. You're sitting on a ticking time bomb that's about to blow your brains out. You're standing on the edge of a cliff and Kilia is gonna shove you to your death. Pick your poison. It's all fucking toxic. It's all one big fuck-up, on both your parts."

By the end of the conversation, I thought I knew what to do. Brendon liked my idea about involving Maria and hauling Kilia's shit to her balcony so that Kilia could retrieve it at her leisure. That way I wouldn't have to face her. And Brendon had been quick to agree with me that I wasn't emotionally tough enough to face Kilia.

I paced for another ten minutes or so and then decided to call Maria. I'd known her long before Kilia had come along and we'd established a good friendship. I hoped she wouldn't interpret my request as pushing the boundaries of that friendship, which might well be the case.

As soon as I picked up my phone, it started ringing.

It was Kilia.

Should I answer it? *No. Yes. No. Yes. No. Yes. No. Aww, fuck.* "Hello?"

"I'm so sorry, baby. Please forgive me."

***

With Kilia sleeping soundly beside me, I laid in bed smoking an e-cigarette, staring out at the moon rising over the black horizon and thinking how great life was again. And even though I still haven't figured out these gentle, ever-caring, pleasure-giving, loving creatures they call women, I decided to give the opposite sex another chance—before packing up my shit once and for all and retreating into the amazon jungle to live like a hermit.

After a two-hour conversation with Kilia last night, I'd agreed to take her back. Never mind that, I hadn't even told her of my plan to kick her out—dump her shit at Maria's and have her pick it up whenever she damn well pleases. No. She'd given an academy-award-winning performance and I was right back in the saddle again. Several apologies, a promise that she would go to her doctor's appointment, get diagnosed, and start taking medication immediately. Hell, she even had a solution for her low sex drive of late. She told me she'd switch to non-lowering-testosterone birth-control pills. She was convinced the new pills would revitalize her sex drive.

I suppose I'm a romantic fool and maybe even an idiot when it comes to love matters. But if nothing else, when I'm on my deathbed, at least I can say I've lived my life with passion.

She'd arrived home a few hours ago filled with pills and filled with glee. Evidently, her colleague at work had been right. Diagnosis—borderline personality disorder. But she had pills for that, and new birth-control pills as well. Of course, I greeted her with a warm smile, a big hug, a kiss, and a glass of water—not necessarily in that order.

She'd swallowed the pills and, without any preamble whatsoever, we headed straight to the bedroom. No dinner, no drinks, no seduction, no foreplay. Just sex. And I have to admit the make-up sex was great. Isn't it always?

I took a few puffs on my e-cigarette, set it down on the nightstand, and studied Kilia. Sleeping peacefully, a satisfied smile on her face. Sleeping Beauty. I was sure she hadn't faked the multiple orgasms. No wonder she was smiling.

Grinning, I got up slowly and silently, careful not to wake her. I hadn't eaten all day and my stomach had begun growling angrily, commanding me into the kitchen. I was also starting to crash from the euphoric energy high, and I could feel heavy fatigue settling in. Thank God tomorrow was Saturday and we could both sleep in after such a tumultuous week.

I wandered into the kitchen, thinking that a peanut butter sandwich would have to do for now. Something, anything, to get the digestion going and shut my stomach up.

The kitchen, a galley-style affair, rather plain really, was cluttered with dishes on the counter and in the sink. We'd both let things slip a little lately, so preoccupied had we been with our own mental health and the health of our relationship. But the roller coaster was going up now, way up, and things could only get better from here.

I opened the fridge and was startled by the sound of my phone ringing. I looked around the dimly lit kitchen and spotted it on the counter, glowing blue with every ring. I thought I had it on silent mode. I always have it on silent mode. *What's going on?*

I answered it without even checking the number.

Brendon skipped all the preliminaries. "You're back in the saddle again, aren't you?"

"I can't talk," I whispered. "Sleeping Beauty is sleeping. I don't wanna wake her."

"Before you hang up, you should know this."

"What?"

"I did a little checking on your little Cinderella."

"What're you talking about?"

"Before she moved to the Island, she lived in Toronto. As coincidence—or divine intervention—would have it, she used to date a friend of mine. Matt Higgins. He kicked her out. You wanna know why?"

I felt cold fear prick the hairs on the back of my neck. I didn't answer. I knew he was gonna tell me anyway.

"She tried to kill him. After he kicked her out, he did a little investigating of his own. And guess what he found?"

"Get to the point," I said, my voice cracking with emotion.

"Three dead exes."

I gasped, frozen to the spot. I tried to speak but no words emerged, just a line of drool dribbling down my chin. I wiped it away with a trembling hand.

A voice, Kilia's voice, startled me.

"What the fuck do you think you're doing?"

I spun around. Kilia stood in the hallway. Unbeknownst to me, she'd crept down the hall, turned the hallway light on, and stood watching me. Her tall frame, silhouetted by the hallway light, appeared black in the dim light.

I put the phone on the counter.

Brendon's tinny-sounding voice: "Are you there, Ted?"

Kilia raised her arm and charged. The hallway light reflected off the silver blade and I caught a glimpse of the metal object—a large butcher knife. I tried to back up, slipped, and she brought the knife down, plunging it deep into my chest. She withdrew it quickly and plunged it into my throat.

I opened my mouth to speak or scream and a stream of blood bubbled up and dribbled down my chin.

I closed my eyes.

Consciousness faded to black.

***

"No, no, no," I shouted, leaping out of bed, and tossing the covers haphazardly on the floor. My heart raced. I struggled to catch my breath, my body glistening with sweat. Even my underwear and T-shirt were sweat-soaked.

A nightmare. Thank God. But, wait. I went to bed naked. I sleep naked. I never sleep in underwear and a T-shirt. What's happening?

My eyes adjusted to the darkness and I began raking my hands over the bed. But the bed was empty. No Kilia.

"Kilia?" I said. "Where are you, honey?"

I hurried out of the bedroom and into the dimly lit kitchen.

My jaw dropped and my eyes popped from their sockets at the macabre scene that confronted me. Kilia was lying on the floor, propped up against the refrigerator, her head tilted to one side. Her chest was covered in blood, covering most of her flimsy white negligee. I knelt down in front of her.

That's when I saw it. A butcher knife protruding from the side of her neck, several tiny rivulets of blood squirting from the wound.

"Baby," I said, overcome with grief and fear. I leaned over and rested my head on her chest. "No, no, no, please God, no."

Thump.... thump..... thump...

I couldn't believe my ears. She had a heartbeat.

I looked into her eyes. They were half-closed and staring at me weakly.

"Hang in there, baby," I said. "I'll call an ambulance." Meanwhile, I thought grimly that if I killed her or tried to kill her I'm fucked now.

She touched my arm lightly, blinked, and a single tear zig-zagged down her cheek. "Help me. Help me, please."

I Can See You

"Why does it sound so strange to you?" Tom Lancing asked his friend Gavin Lavine. "I mean, the CIA used remote viewing in 1975 to spy on the Russians."

"I've just never heard of it before," Gavin said. "Explain how it works."

Tom looked around the park that Saturday afternoon. It was a glorious, sunny day in Montague, PEI, and he'd deliberately picked a remote location. They sat at a picnic table at least a hundred feet from other tables positioned around a snack bar. About a dozen people occupied the snack bar tables, drinking coffee, eating ice cream, chatting, and enjoying their Saturday in the sun. Tom made sure no one was looking at them before continuing. He was probably a little paranoid about his gift; however, to his mind, his caution and suspicion were totally justified.

"It's essentially a discipline of the paranormal or parapsychology," Tom said. "You train your mind, bring it to a higher state of consciousness whereby you can see things, see people, thousands of miles away, for example. While you're in this kind of meditative state, you're capable of remote viewing. In the case of the CIA's Stargate Project, they were training psychic spies basically."

"What happened to the Stargate Project?" Gavin asked.

"The twenty million dollar project was shut down in 1995. Apparently, the CIA claimed it was a failure and they couldn't gather any actionable intelligence. If you believe that it really was a failure, I've got some swamp land to sell you."

"I'm just skeptical, that's all," Gavin said, running a hand through his scruffy beard and adjusting his black baseball cap sideways, the way he generally preferred to wear it.

As if taking a cue, Tom removed his blue baseball cap, ran a hand through his long, wavy brown hair, and replaced the cap. "Well, I too cherish a healthy amount of skepticism about government. But, we're getting sidetracked. I wanted to tell you about my remote viewing experience recently."

Gavin watched a woman pushing a baby stroller in the distance before turning to Tom. "Okay, go for it."

Tom wasn't sure how much to say. He'd had psychic abilities for as long as he could remember. As a youngster, the phone would ring and he'd know who it was before anyone answered. Even though he'd known little about psychic phenomena at the time, he'd tried to develop his God-given talents. And in large part, he'd succeeded. His brother bought a new car. He told him what color it was before he even saw it. His sister bought him a gift. He told her what was inside the box before he'd opened it. He used to tell his mother what she was planning for dinner even before she'd gone grocery shopping. It was as if he could read her mind. As an adult, Tom spent more time on the remote viewing aspect of his psychic abilities. He completed several meditation courses, read everything he could get his hands on, and had reached a point where it had become perfectly natural to him to meditate, open up his consciousness to the world, steer that energy and awareness to a particular geographic area and, in short order, he'd start seeing, sketching, and writing down the results. Last night, he'd focused his mind on Gavin. And he had to admit, he was a little disturbed at what he saw. *How to put this gently? First, see if he lies. He will.*

"What did you do last night?"

Gavin's face reddened, imperceptible to most, but readily visible to Tom's finely tuned extra-sensory perception.

"What does this have to do with me?" Gavin said, his eyes narrowing.

"I hope you don't think I'm prying, but I remotely viewed you last night."

"That's creepy."

"I didn't intend to," Tom lied. "It just came to me."

"What came to you?"

"No, no. I asked you first. What did you do last night?"

"Watched a couple of movies. Fuck all, really."

"Okay. And what did you do after that?"

"Went to bed?"

"Before that."

Gavin searched Tom's eyes intently, trying to see how much Tom knew. But Tom's eyes revealed nothing.

"Where's this going?" Gavin said.

"Nowhere if you don't want it to."

"I don't want it to," Gavin said. "I watched two movies, had a snack, and went to bed. That's it, that's all. If you saw something different you're gonna have to tell me."

"Okay," Tom said, tired of beating around the bush. "After watching TV, you printed a picture from your computer. Then you took the picture and pinned it to a dart board. Then you threw darts at the image, hitting it in the face multiple times. And I saw you pulling out a baseball bat from your closet and practicing a few swings. What was that all about? Who was that picture of? More importantly, what're you planning on doing to them?"

The color drained from Gavin's face. He placed two muscular forearms on the picnic table and leaned toward Tom, face tightening, fists clenching. "You shouldn't be doing that. You shouldn't be doing that. Prying into people's lives like that."

Gavin's reaction was exactly what Tom had been worried about. That Gavin would act on his impulses. They'd been friends for over a decade. Gavin's violent temper had caused a break-up in his relationship soon after Tom had met him. Giselle, his wife at the time, had to get a restraining order to keep him away and there was still some controversy surrounding whether Gavin had actually laid a hand on her or not. A few things were clear, however. After one violent outburst, the cops arrived. Gavin's belongings had been tossed curbside and he'd been forced to move out and find his own apartment. Eventually, charges had been dropped, or so the story went. After getting fired from his construction job, Gavin attended group anger management sessions and found a new job as a butcher at Sobeys. It appeared he was on the road to rebuilding his life, and bettering his personality. Growing and maturing as a person. But now this. Had the rage demons seized control of his psyche again? Tom didn't know, but he had heard rumors that even prior to Gavin assaulting Giselle—verbally or otherwise—that he'd had other brushes with the law during his adolescence.

"Listen, I was only trying to help," Tom said. "I'm your friend, remember? Tell me what the problem is. Maybe I *can* help."

Gavin put his head in his hands and slumped onto the tabletop.

Tom watched him silently.

Finally, Gavin looked Tom directly in the eye, his expression pained.

"It's my boss at Sobeys. The picture I printed was of my boss. He keeps harping on me about every little thing and it's driving me nuts."

"Well, the dart-board-thing disturbed me. And the baseball bat disturbed me even more."

"I like to think I was just getting out my frustrations, you know. But I don't know. I have to admit, at one point I felt like smashing Brent Shanihan's head in with that bat. And I even started planning it."

"Don't do it."

"Shit, man, I can't believe you saw all that stuff. It's creepy. I mean, can you see me beating off and stuff like that."

"Trust me, that's something I wouldn't want to see, so I wouldn't see."

"You can control this... remote viewing, as you call it?"

"For the most part, yeah. Although sometimes the images are stronger than at other times. And sometimes I get nothing at all."

"How do you do it?"

"I was born with it. But over the years, I've developed it. Read tons of stuff, watched a hundred videos and documentaries. I've even talked to a few people who can also do it."

Gavin removed his cap and wiped a sweaty forehead. "Can you see into the future?"

"I don't think so, but I believe that's possible. Well, for sure it's possible with clairvoyants and the like. But I read that a guy who participated in the Stargate Project made a killing on the stock market by being able to see what the stocks would do in the future. More than one guy apparently."

"Wow, that's crazy."

Indeed it was rather mind-blowing for some people, Tom thought. But he also realized Gavin, as he so often did, was steering him off topic. He'd met up with him essentially to warn him to calm the fuck down, control his temper, and don't go doing anything stupid. But to get to that point he had to figure out what else was bothering Gavin. Tom had seen a collage of other more alarming images at the end of his remote viewing session last night. Gavin threatening his mirror, putting on his best I'll-fuck-you-up face. Gavin punching the wall. Gavin, in a rage, storming around his apartment cursing and swearing. He hadn't told him the whole story yet for fear of retribution or, worse still, losing a friend. He decided in that instant he wasn't gonna tell Gavin the whole truth. His abridged revelations earlier had already brought Gavin close to the boiling point. No point in turning up the heat.

"I'm used to it," Tom said. "For me, it's just a part of life. I try to use it to help people. Which reminds me, that's what I'm doing here. You're not gonna do anything stupid are you?"

"No."

"You sure?"

"Yeah."

"Is that all that's bothering you? Your boss?"

Gavin paused, shifting his gaze to the manicured lawn.

A tell, Tom thought. *He won't make eye contact.* "Come on, bro. We've been bros a long time. I hope we'll always be bros. Tell me your problems and I'll send you a whopping bill later for shrinking your head."

"Fuck you."

"Seriously, what's on your mind?"

Gavin sighed, and after a long pause, said, "A few things. Ever since that nasty mess with my ex I've been ex-communicated in this town. As soon as I start getting close to a woman they go and do some checking on me, learn of my checkered past, and want nothing to do with me. I was just starting to get close to Cheryl—you know, the one who works at the carwash—and I guess she started asking about me and that. So two days ago, I go in there to ask for the big date and it went over like a lead balloon. I mean she'd been warming up to me for months now. Got my confidence all built up only to get shattered."

"What did she say?"

Gavin's face flushed and he gripped the edge of the table with both meat hooks, digging his nails into the surface. "I'm paraphrasing here, but basically she said I don't go out with wife beaters."

"That sucks. Sorry to hear it. But don't worry, bro. They'll be others."

Gavin's face contorted and he lifted the edge of the picnic table a good two inches off the grass before releasing it. "Others? What others? This fucking small town has barely over two thousand residents. And by now, they all know all about me. And I'll tell you something, because you're probably wondering. I never laid a hand on Giselle. Not one fucking pinky finger. Sure, I had a problem with amphetamines at the time, and I know I didn't treat her that well. But hell, I've been to anger management group therapy, anger management private counselling, drug addiction group therapy, and even drug addiction private counselling. I'm clean, man. I've been off the pills for almost a decade now. I don't use any substances at all. I've tried to reform my life and where did it get me? Right fucking back to square one."

Gavin slammed his fist down on the picnic table, delivering an exclamation point to his confessions.

"I don't think you're at square one at all," Tom said. "You've come a hell of a long way and I'm proud of you."

Gavin wiped his moistening eyes and looked at Tom, deep pain, frustration, and sadness imprinted in his blue eyes. "Thanks, bro. I appreciate it. I really do. But, damn, I want a girlfriend. I need a girlfriend. I mean, I'm not sure you know what it's like. You've been with Mirabel for almost three years now. You've got a good relationship, you're self-employed, in a job you like, with that freelance editor gig, and you've got it made. I mean, in the sense that you're happy."

"I have my ups and downs. Why don't we go the Charlottetown next weekend? We'll rent a hotel and do some bar-hopping. That way we don't have to worry about drunk driving. It's only a half hour away and Charlottetown has way more people. Way more selection. Maybe that's far enough away to escape the gossip grapevine."

Gavin smiled wanly, and for the first time that afternoon, Tom saw a small twinkle in the big man's eyes.

"You want to?" Gavin asked. "What about Mirabel?"

"She's going to Moncton next weekend to visit her mom. She'll be gone the entire weekend. And even if she was here, she wouldn't mind. She trusts me."

Gavin extended his mitt. "Let's shake on that."

They did.

Tom said, "I want you to promise me you won't go doing anything stupid in the meantime. I want to help you. If things don't work out in Charlottetown, maybe I'll ask my girlfriend if she has a friend for you. But, I need your word first."

"You have my word."

"Shake on it," Tom said.

They did.

For the next fifteen or so minutes, they discussed less explosive topics. The weather. Sports. Gavin's surprisingly good relationship with his mother and father, sister, and brother. Tom was careful not to broach any potentially hurtful subjects. He'd learned more about his friend in the last hour than he had in ten years. He knew it took a lot of effort for Gavin to come clean about his personal demons.

They rose and began walking to their respective vehicles. Before they parted, Gavin said, "Are you sure your remote viewing of me was unintentional?"

"No, actually I told a white lie. I was worried about you so I called up those images in real time."

"I thought so," Gavin said. "Can you do me a favor and try not to do that in the future? It freaks me out."

"I'll try."

***

A week later. Saturday evening. They sat in a booth at The Pilot House, a popular old-English style pub in downtown Charlottetown. Located in a turn-of-the-century heritage building, it exuded a cozy and rustic charm. It was crowded with weekend revelers and the volume level was high. But it was a soothing sound to Tom: enthusiastic voices, and plenty of laughter.

Tom was impressed by the change in Gavin's appearance. He'd gotten a haircut, trimmed his beard into a neat little goatee, abandoned the baseball cap, and even purchased some new duds, a new pair of black denim Levi jeans, and a blue denim Levi shirt. The burly man cleaned up quite well.

Tom had stayed true to his word—if he had even given his word—and had not pried into Gavin's troubled life. He had, however, put out random remote viewing searches in the hope of finding a soulmate for his friend.

And, coincidentally or not, he'd stumbled upon a mousy little dark-haired woman rummaging around her apartment for the perfect outfit while at the same time lamenting about her dismal love life. Talking to herself really, but Tom wasn't about to hold that against her. Something about the randomness of it—destiny perhaps—told him she would be the perfect match for Gavin.

Tom took a swill of his draft and glanced around the bar. Lo and behold, there she was, sitting in a corner alone, a pint of draft beer her only companion. Tom had already filled Gavin in on the vision—if you want to call it that—and his friend was over the moon with excitement.

"Holy shit, you're not gonna believe this," Tom said. "Don't look now, but I see her. Right behind you—in the corner. Twelve o'clock."

"Are you kidding me?" Gavin asked, swinging around and staring straight at her.

"I told you not to look now, idiot."

But it was too late. She'd glanced up furtively from staring into the white sudsy abyss of her libation, looked straight at Gavin, and then looked away immediately.

"It's too late," Gavin said, turning around. "She spotted me."

"Well, then. What're you gonna do about it?"

"I'm gonna approach her right now and ask her if she wants to join us for a drink."

"You kidding me? You don't need any liquid confidence?"

"Alcohol has never been one of my vices. You know that."

"I was kidding."

Before Tom could say more, Gavin strode confidently over to her table. Tom watched as Gavin struck up a conversation with the woman who Tom thought strongly resembled Rocky's wife, Adrian, in the Rocky movies. Talia Shire, he believed her name was.

In no time, Gavin slid back her chair chivalrously and accompanied her to their booth.

"This is my friend, Tom," Gavin said, waving her into the booth.

She climbed in, scooted across, and offered her hand to Tom. "I'm Sylvia," she said. "Sylvia Squires. Nice to meet you."

Tom took the hand and shook it. Her hand was trembling. *What's she afraid of? I hope not us.*

They started off with a few ice-breakers. Admissions that they were all born and bred on the Island, how much they loved it, and what a gorgeous summer they were enjoying. A little talk about Charlottetown and how charming the small city was with its old-fashioned architecture and robust community spirit.

Sylvia had begun the conversation tentatively. She looked nervous. But the more they talked, the more she warmed up to them, especially to Gavin.

It didn't take long for Gavin to switch the conversation to relationships. "Are you waiting for someone? Or are you here by yourself?"

"I'm here by myself," Sylvia said. "My friend, Rita, was supposed to come, but she's got the flu."

"Sorry to hear that," Gavin said. "You didn't have anyone else to call? Sorry, I didn't mean it that way. It sounds like I'm saying you don't have any other friends, but I didn't mean it like that at all. Shit, I'm just sticking my foot deeper and deeper inside my yap. I should quit while I'm ahead. Sorry."

Sylvia laughed nervously. "Don't worry about it. I do have other friends in town. Most of them are married. Rita and I made this plan a week ago, but she called me yesterday and told me she was sick."

"Oh, you're single?" Gavin said.

Sylvia glanced nervously out the window for a moment. "Yeah, about three years now. How about you?"

"Hate to admit it, but, yeah, for many years now," Gavin said.

To Tom, Sylvia said, "And you?"

"I'm happily in a relationship," Tom said. "My girlfriend's visiting family in Moncton this weekend."

"Oh shit," Sylvia said, watching a big man enter the bar and bee-line it straight toward them.

"What?" Gavin asked. "What's wrong?"

"That's Stanley, my ex. A bit of a wing-nut."

Stanley, about six-foot-five and roughly 250 pounds, arrived at their booth and scowled at Sylvia, rubbing a hand over his bald head and then gliding it down his clean-shaven face.

"Hi Sylvia," he said. "I see you've found some new friends."

She didn't bother introducing them. "Yes."

Stanley's beady eyes darted over to Gavin. "Is he your new boyfriend?"

"That's none of your business," she said.

"Oh, but it *is* my business. You told me you didn't want a relationship with anyone anymore. Now you're with these two clowns."

Tom watched Gavin grip the underside of the table, his eyes contracting into slits.

"That was three years ago, Stanley," Sylvia said. "Things change."

"No, they don't. The more things change the more they stay the same. I wanted you three years ago and I still want you now."

"Well, you can't have me," Sylvia said, her face flushing. "When are you gonna get that through your head?"

"What's with you?" Stanley said, his dark eyes drilling into Gavin. "Someone shit in your cornflakes?"

Gavin stood quickly, coming face-to-face with Stanley. His imposing size and weight was at least equal to Stanley's physicality.

"Why don't you leave us alone?" Gavin said. "You fucking clown."

"What'd you call me?" Stanley said.

"I called you the same thing you called us. A fucking clown. Well, maybe I added the F-bomb, but a little embellishment never hurt anyone."

In an instant, Stanley grabbed Gavin by the shirt collar, shoving him against the table. Gavin pushed him off. Stanley swung a roundhouse right fist. Gavin ducked, cocked his fists, and advanced.

In seconds, two burly bouncers raced over and grabbed Stanley, one on each arm.

"Let's go," one said. "They were sitting peacefully here and you're causing trouble. Now you're leaving."

"I didn't start it," Stanley said. "I just came over to say hi and this fucking clown started bad-mouthing me."

"That's not what happened," Sylvia said, pointing at her ex. "He started it."

"I know who started it," the bouncer said, beginning to escort Stanley out the door. "I saw everything."

"You'll get yours," Stanley said to Gavin as he neared the door. Glaring at his ex, he added, "And so will you, bitch."

"Shut your pie-hole and fuck off," Gavin said. "You can land in jail for threatening people like that."

"When I finish with you you'll wish you were in jail," Stanley said.

A helpful patron held the door open while both bouncers heaved Stanley outside.

Peering through the window, Tom saw an animated conversation ensue, but he couldn't hear what they were saying. Finally, he saw Stanley turn around and trudge down the street, his head down, his shoulders slumped.

"Is that guy sane?' Tom asked.

"I don't think so," Sylvia said. "He's an unstable alcoholic with an explosive temper. That's why I got rid of him."

"Will he make good on his threats?" Gavin asked.

"I don't think so," Sylvia said. "He never has before. But you never know."

"He's threatened you before?" Gavin said."

Sylvia nodded.

"Has he ever laid a hand on you?" Gavin asked.

"Once," Sylvia said. "Gave me a black eye one night while he was in a drunken stupor. I dumped him after that. Thank God I never let him move in with me."

"Does he, like, stalk you?' Tom asked.

"He's showed up a little too coincidentally a few times in places I frequent."

Tom was going to follow it up with other questions. Did you press charges? If not, why? But he stopped himself. The situation with Stanley and Sylvia was eerily similar to the relationship Gavin had had with Giselle, his ex. Tom didn't want to make Gavin feel uncomfortable. On the contrary, he had his friend's best interests at heart.

"I don't believe in coincidences," Gavin said. "He sounds like a nutcase to me."

"By the way," Sylvia said. "Thanks for intervening."

"It was nothing," Gavin said. "I was just thinking, if you live around here, maybe I should walk you home. You know, just to be safe."

"I rent an apartment a few blocks away from here," Sylvia said. "But I'll be fine."

"Did you drive here?"

"No. I walked."

Tom could see where this was going and he thought it was time for him to bow out. The Quality Inn was mere blocks from The Pilot House, so they hadn't bothered to bring Tom's Ford Explorer. Right on cue, Gavin kicked him in the shin just hard enough to activate their pre-arranged signal for, "Get the fuck out of here and gimme some one-on-one time with this woman."

"I insist," Gavin said. "How could I live with myself if I didn't and something happened to you?"

"Nothing will happen to me," Sylvia said. But her eyes told a different story. She was scared. She wanted protection.

"Are you sure?" Gavin asked.

"No, I'm not sure, actually. I think I'll take you up on that offer."

"Great," Gavin said. "Should I order another round of drinks?"

"I'll have one more," Sylvia said. "That scene with me ex rattled me a bit and I don't wanna stay too long."

"On that note," Tom said, "I think I'll head back to the hotel. It's still early enough for me to call my Mirabel and not get my ass chewed off for not calling when I said I would."

***

Sipping a decaffeinated coffee in his room at the Quality Inn about an hour later, Tom wondered if he should call Gavin.

No, it's only been an hour. But, what if he's in trouble? He can look after himself. You're not his mother. Let him have his fun. I don't know.

During a conversation with Mirabel earlier, he'd explained to her what had happened and she had sounded alarmed. A university student majoring in psychology, she thought Stanley showed all the signs of acting out with explosive violence. He'd already demonstrated half a dozen psychological disorders, according to Mirabel.

The more Tom thought about it, the more he realized he had to do something. So he did what any skilled remote viewer would do. He pulled out his trusty notepad and pen, dimmed the lights, sat at the hotel suite desk, and closed his eyes. He slowly went through the meditative exercise of first calming his mind, then blanking it, opening it up to signals and signs from what he viewed as the greater consciousness.

Five minutes later, a smattering of images began flooding his mind. Then the multiple images distilled into one scene—Gavin and Sylvia talking on the sidewalk outside of a burgundy 19th century two-story home.

"Are you gonna be okay?" Gavin said.

"I'm a little scared, but I'll be fine."

"Are you sure?"

"Yes... no, I'm not sure."

"Do you want me to come in and stay for a while?"

"Okay."

Tom watched them enter the house. He opened his eyes, made a note of the number, 32, and closed them again. He had to get the street name in case he needed it. Magically his eyes floated down the street, collecting information. He stopped at the street sign—Green Street—opened his eyes and wrote it down, and closed them again.

But instead of returning to the house—Tom's green eyes stopped and began following a black pickup truck that had just turned onto the street. The truck parked near Sylvia's house and the driver killed the ignition. Tom's eyes floated outside the truck, trying to see inside. But it was too dark. His eyes easily penetrated the passenger window and he found his remote viewing consciousness right next to Stanley, gripping the steering wheel and seething with rage.

"Fucking bitch wants to blow me off in front of her new boyfriend, does she? Well, I'll fucking show her."

Then Stanley produced a handgun, kissed the barrel, and got out of the truck.

Tom opened his eyes instantly, immediately snapping out of his state of higher consciousness. He scrambled across the room, dove on the bed, grabbed his phone, and speed-dialed Gavin. Four rings later, it went to voicemail.

"Take Sylvia and run," Tom said. "He's got a gun... Stanley's got a gun."

He stuffed his phone in his pocket, grabbed his keys, and rushed out the door. He skipped the elevator, raced down two flights of stairs, and exited the building, fueled by adrenaline. His mind was racing and he was on the verge of panic by the time he reached the parking lot.

32 Green Street. Not far from the hotel. Should I run or take the Explorer? Run. Take the car. Run. Wait. Call the cops. Call 911.

But Tom skipped the 911 call, deciding that time was of the essence. Instead, he got in his car and drove the seven blocks to 32 Green Street. Three minutes later, he arrived—white-faced, white-knuckled, and sweat-soaked.

***

Knock, knock.

"I wonder who that could be," Sylvia said.

"Are you expecting anyone?" Gavin said, feeling a dreadfully cold chill on the nape of his neck. Ever since that incident with Stanley he'd been on edge, half-expecting the lunatic to show up at any time with deadly intentions. Maybe his hunches weren't so far wrong.

"No, I'm not."

Gavin grabbed her wrist. "Don't answer it. Let's look out the window first."

The color drained from her face. "Okay."

They approached the window, pulled the blinds aside, and peered out. Even in the suffused light, Gavin could identify the man. The bulky frame was unmistakable. Stanley, whatever the fuck his last name was.

Knock, knock.

Before Gavin realized it, Sylvia hurried to the door, peered out the peephole, and said, "Go away. Leave me alone for once and let me have a life."

Stanley's voice, from the other side of the door: "Open up. I just wanna talk."

"No. Go home. I don't wanna talk. You can't come here uninvited any time you want. Go away."

Gavin was about to leave the window, pull Sylvia away from the door, step outside and knock some sense into Stanley, when suddenly Stanley appeared in front of the window and glared at him. Then he pulled a gun from his trench coat pocket and aimed it at Gavin.

***

As soon as Tom pulled up to the house, he saw Stanley pull out a gun and point it at the bay window. *Oh fuck, no.*

A shadowy figure standing on the inside of the window, who could only be Gavin, ducked. Another person, Sylvia—*must be Sylvia*—ran to his aid. They both dove out of sight.

Kaplow!

The bullet shattered the window. A front porch light went on two doors down from 32 Green Street. A dog started barking.

Then Stanley pointed the gun at the front door and fired two shots.

Kaplow! Kaplow!

Then he kicked the bullet-damaged door open.

Tom was way past thinking now. He reacted solely on instinct, pressing the gas pedal to the floor and steering hard right. He barreled over the curb and as he neared the wooden front porch, Stanley swung around and fired a single shot.

Kaplow!

As Tom ducked, the bullet smashed through the front windshield and exited through the rear windshield.

The silver Ford Explorer rammed into the porch step, splintered wood, and then rocketed up onto the porch, slamming into Stanley, and smashing right through the house and into the living room. As Tom braked, the Explorer skidded across the living room floor, and crashed, pinning Stanley against a partially demolished wall.

Tom killed the ignition and climbed out of the vehicle.

Stanley's upper torso was slumped over the hood of the vehicle, both arms outstretched. He still held the gun. Debris particles, blood and guts, clung to his neck, arms, back and head. A pool of blood fanned out around him.

Sylvia and Gavin appeared out of a cloud of dust.

"Holy fuck," Gavin said. "I think you killed him."

"You saved our lives," Sylvia said.

"I could've killed you guys too," Tom said, feeling guilty. "Are you okay?"

They nodded in unison.

Suddenly, Tom heard a metal-on-metal scraping sound.

All eyes focused on Stanley's hand, still clutching the gun. He raised his bloodied and battered head, looked at them, and put the barrel of the gun to his temple.

"Don't," Sylvia shouted.

"I can see you," Stanley said.

Then he pulled the trigger and blew his brains out.

Kaplow!!!

Meaningless

Terry Weathers and his friend Linda Johnson wandered through the forest on Terry's property on a sunny fall afternoon. They were enjoying the fresh air, beautiful fall colors, and the magic that only Mother Nature delivers. They were talking about anything and everything that popped into their minds, keeping the conversation light and playful.

They stopped at a fork in the road. One way led to the beach, the other, to another recreation site that Terry had carved out of the forest.

"Which way?" Terry asked.

"Let's go to the Caribbean North site," Linda said. "I like that spot."

"Okay," Terry said. "We can always circle back to the beach later if you want."

They carried on.

"Did you hear what happened to Theresa at her dinner party?" Terry asked. Theresa Brice was a mutual friend of theirs. They'd both cancelled their invitations to the party, on account of they were less than pleased with one of Theresa's friends. One Chad Smithers, a conspiracy theorist and downright arrogant son of a bitch.

Linda was walking behind him. "No."

"She slipped on her porch and fell."

"Really? Is she okay?"

"Not really. She broke her leg in three places."

"Wow. Sorry to hear that."

"I know. I hope she has a speedy recovery. Do you know, if I had decided to go to that party I probably could've prevented that."

"What do you mean?"

"I mean if I was there I would've changed the trajectory of events leading up to her fall. I might've been pouring her a glass of wine or even talking to her at the time. Either way, if I had been there, it might not have happened. Or, even if you went, for example, it probably wouldn't have happened."

"What difference does that line of thought make?" Linda asked. "It *did* happen."

"I just mean it in the context of how if one person enters your life at a particular time, or a certain event occurs, it will change the course of your life forever. You know, like if you're driving to the store, and you meet a friend on the way and chat for five minutes, only to discover when you arrive at the store that it's just been held up at gunpoint and two people are dead. Then you realize that could've been you, but the unintentional intervention of your friend save your life."

"Well, I think your point is meaningless," Linda said in an agitated tone.

Terry stopped and turned around, a dark shadow enveloping him. He looked at Linda. She was clearly angry. *She's the one who's offended. Really?*

"I don't think it's meaningless at all," Terry said. "On the contrary, I think it's meaningful to have these discussions. Saying it's meaningless means you don't respect my opinion. You're entitled to disagree with my opinion, but I would've hoped that at least you'd respect it, as I do yours. You could've said I don't agree with your opinion but I respect it."

Linda avoided the issue of disrespect, instead choosing to put out the fire with gasoline. "Don't be so sensitive. You go off on these rants a lot. And sometimes they don't make any sense. This is one of them in my opinion."

A sudden gust of wind blew in. The treetops started swaying and hissing. Above, a bank of clouds rolled in, obliterating the bright sunshine.

Terry fired back. "You're entitled to your opinion, but I'm not entitled to agree with it. I'm a fiction writer, for fuck sakes, and maybe I was just thinking out loud to come up with another story idea, for all you know."

"Here we go again. Another story idea. I suppose I'm gonna be some character and you'll cleverly disguise me as someone else so you can work out your frustrations through your words."

"In fact, my words are a kind of therapy," Terry said. "And maybe I *will* do that. Who the fuck knows?"

They started walking again. Terry hoped the exercise would go some way to dissolving the anger boiling up inside him. He picked up his pace, increasing the distance between them.

"You keep up that profanity and I'm leaving," Linda said.

"It wasn't directed at you."

"Like hell it wasn't."

"Okay, calm down," Terry said. He thought he knew how to dial down the heat. Right or wrong, just apologize and admit defeat. Life was too short to spend it ranting, raving, and raging. Linda thought his point was meaningless. He couldn't change that if he whacked her upside the head with a baseball bat. "I'm sorry. Let's change the subject. We don't wanna upset Mother Nature. Ever since we started this, the wind's picked up and now the clouds have annihilated the sun. Let's quit while we're ahead."

"Fair enough," Linda said. "But don't be silly. Mother Nature doesn't hear people arguing. Jesus Christ, it's just a forest. And you started it..."

As a powerful gust of wind swept in, Terry heard a thunderous crack. Now a good thirty feet ahead of Linda, he spun around.

A large spruce tree, uprooted by the powerful wind gust, came crashing down, smashing Linda in the head, and slamming her onto the forest carpet.

She didn't have a chance to look up. She didn't have a chance to step out of the way. She didn't even have a chance to scream.

"Ooooph!" was all she managed to say as the large timber mashed her skull and shattered it into a million pieces of blood, guts, brain matter, and gore.

Terry approached her dead body. Jaw-dropped, he studied it for a full minute. "That shut you up once and for all."

Then he shed a single tear, wiped it away, and continued on his werifesteria tour, whistling the tune to John Denver's song, *I've Been Working on the Railroad.*

Alien Abduction

"You should see *Close Encounters of the Fifth Kind*," Mark Waters said. "It's powerful and convincing. Changed the way I think about consciousness, our purpose on the planet, government secrecy, and secret agendas."

"The whole thing is bunk," Sheila Samuelson said. "That stupid documentary. I checked out the 20-second trailer and couldn't even make it through that. It's not something I'm interested in, would watch, or would even buy into for that matter."

"Well, you're entitled to your opinion, and I respect that, but before you go dissing it you should at least see it first. How do you know it's bunk if you've never seen it?"

"I don't need to see it," Sheila said. "UFOs are fake. Simple as that."

"I don't think so," Mark said. "When I was in university I wrote a research paper on UFOs and extraterrestrials. Almost a year in the making. My conclusion was that the overwhelming amount of evidence—UFO sightings, and alien abductions—strongly supports the notion that other civilizations exist. That documentary validates and supports many of the conclusions I came to a long time ago. There is just too much out there to ignore."

"Well, I'm sure my conspiracy-theory-believing sister would be interested," Sheila said with a laugh.

Mark sipped his coffee and frowned. They were on their lunch break, sitting at a Starbucks in downtown Charlottetown. Mark had thought long and hard before deciding to broach the subject with Sheila. He had thought they had a lot in common. And they did, actually. Both not too hard on the eyes. Both in their mid-thirties. Both single. Both software designers at Greentech, a large Canadian software manufacturing company. They'd even studied at the same tech college, loved the outdoors, reading, cooking, and intellectual challenges. He thought this discussion would at least challenge Sheila to look into the subject of UFOs before dismissing it out of hand without offering any evidence to support her opinion. But it had backfired like a misfired hand grenade and blown his legs out from under him. It was time to diffuse the situation before the next hand grenade decapitated him.

"Hey, I get that a lot of people aren't gonna buy into it," Mark said. "Probably most people wouldn't believe it, actually."

"I've seen many so-called UFO sightings get debunked by scientists as hoaxes," Sheila said.

Hmm. Maybe she does have evidence after all. "I'm sure a lot of them are fake," Mark said. "I think we should agree to disagree on this one and leave it alone. It's up to you to look at more recent data or not."

"Or not," Sheila said adamantly.

***

Maybe it was some subconscious inclination to want to believe Mark. Maybe it was just intellectual curiosity. Or maybe it was just her way of winding down after a stressful day at work. Sheila didn't know. But later that Monday night, she found herself sitting on the balcony of her downtown apartment gazing up into the sky. Star gazing. She had her binoculars pressed tightly to her eyes and she wandered from one star to the next, trying to detect movement. *No you're not. You're simply stargazing. It relaxes you. Nothing more. Nothing less.*

About an hour later, she had worked herself into a deep state of relaxation, a kind of tranquil connectedness with the galaxy. And it was as if some unacknowledged, unknown, or undiscovered part of her consciousness had begun to take over, asking the same questions over and over: *"Are you out there? If you are, will you show me a sign?"*

Then suddenly she saw it. A large yellow cylindrical object flying right toward her. She removed the binoculars from her eyes as it zoomed toward her, circled quickly over the downtown skyline, and then stopped in midflight, less than a thousand feet from her.

"Holy shit, are you for real?"

As if in response, it flashed three times and then disappeared.

Exactly three minutes later, Sheila had Mark on the phone. She could barely contain her excitement.

"I should never have doubted you, Mark," she said. "Please accept my apology. You're not gonna believe this but I just saw a UFO. Right over downtown, then practically right in front of my balcony."

"I *do* believe you," Mark said. "Please, gimme the details."

Sheila explained the events leading up to the sighting and then the actual sighting. "It was almost as if I summoned it."

"I think we both summoned it, actually."

"What? Did you see it too?"

"Yeah."

"Tell me more."

"Okay, but you need more background information first. You need to get educated on this. Watch *Close Encounters of the Fifth Kind*. I'll come over on Saturday night and we'll see if we can see it again."

A few hours later, Sheila had to admit that she was blown away by the overwhelming amount of evidence in the documentary. Presented by Doctor Steven Greer, a retired trauma doctor and authority on UFOs, the documentary presented compelling video and photographic evidence, secret government files, and powerful interviews of well-respected and prominent figures. It also revealed that Greer had briefed and routinely briefs US presidents and intelligence officials on ET phenomenon. The founder of a grassroots movement to peaceably contact extraterrestrials, he and his group have summoned, contacted, and communicated with numerous aliens, according to the documentary.

The big lie, Greer claimed, is that the US government wants people to believe that extraterrestrials have hostile intentions in order to use fear to manipulate and control the population. But, according to Greer, quite the contrary is true. If anything, the ETs view humans as hostile and, with their advanced technology, if they wanted to destroy our planet and civilization, they would've done it a long time ago.

Greer maintained that long-forgotten spiritual knowledge holds the key to humans peacefully contacting advanced ET civilizations, which he claimed are numerous. Accompanied by a group of followers on an ET contacting field trip, Greer even documented in compelling fashion how one man's hearing was restored by these highly advanced and mysterious beings.

Wow, Sheila thought, reaching the end of her notes. *Contact has begun. For thousands of people around the world, contact has begun.*

***

Saturday evening. Sheila's apartment balcony. In spite of the city lights, the stars and moon glowed ominously. Mark and Sheila had already been discussing UFOs and ETs for well over an hour. Mark was impressed by the research Sheila had done. She'd vetted and read everything she could find online from credible sources. She'd even watched *Sirius* and *Unacknowledged*, two UFO documentaries prominently featuring Steven Greer and his work.

"I have to admit, this is life-changing stuff," Sheila said. "How long have you been studying it?"

"I saw a UFO when I was fifteen," Mark said. "Ever since then, I've been a part-time scholar of UFOs. But, within the last three years, my interest has skyrocketed, especially after reading and seeing the ground-breaking work of Steven Greer."

"What happened when you saw the UFO? Describe the sighting."

"I was walking on the beach one night. I stopped and sat down to enjoy the stars and the moon. It was a beautiful fall evening. I started daydreaming about what it would be like to live on Mars, started inventing all these aliens in my head, and then all of a sudden, wham! This cylindrical yellow disk comes soaring out of the sky, circles three times around the calm waters in front of me, and then shoots off and disappears into the stars. I'm talking super-fast."

"Wow," Sheila said. "I wouldn't have believed it if I didn't see it myself. The other big question I have—especially after seeing all these people summoning and contacting ETs—is this: Did you summon the UFO I saw?"

"Actually, I think I did," Mark said. "I figured the only way I could convince you is if you saw one. But, from what you say, it sounds to me like we both summoned it."

"Should we try again?"

"You read my mind. I thought that was the reason we were here."

"I suppose you're right. I'll take your cue."

Mark and Sheila spread some throw rugs out on the balcony, lit a single candle, and placed it on a small table in front of them. Then, following Mark's instructions, they sat cross-legged in front of the candle and closed their eyes.

"Now totally blank your mind," Mark said.

"Okay," Sheila said.

"When it's blank, let me know and I'll tell you what to do next."

"Okay."

They sat silently for a few minutes and then Sheila said, "I'm drawing a blank."

"Okay," Mark said. "So am I. Now, I want you to repeat these things over and over again in your mind. Advanced beings, we come in peace. We mean you no harm. We wish to learn about your civilization and tell you about ours. Please contact us."

"Can we say it out loud a few times, so I remember it?"

"Sure."

They repeated the sentences three times, closed their eyes, silent and still. Mark had tried on numerous occasions to contact extraterrestrials and he wondered if they would find success this time around. He'd only ever had success twice in his life; once three years ago, and the second time last week, when he'd wanted to bring Sheila around to his way of thinking.

Three minutes passed.

Nothing.

"How will we know when to open our eyes?" Sheila asked.

"You'll feel it," Mark said. "You'll feel them."

They meditated for a few more minutes, silently entreating the ETs to contact them.

Mark began to lose track of the time. He'd reached a point of ultra-deep meditation where he could see through closed eyes the beauty of the moon, the stars, and the whole magnificent and mysterious galaxy.

It was Sheila who snapped him out of this reverie. "Do you feel that?"

He kept his eyes closed, opening his senses to the larger consciousness. Then he *did* feel it. A satisfying warmth starting at the base of his spine and shooting up to the nape of his neck, filling him with inexplicably soothing heat. More than that, a sense of comfort, peace, and happiness.

But it disappeared in a flash and was replaced by a stern and authoritative voice: "Pay attention, earthlings. I'll only say this once. You recklessly destroy your planet and yourselves. If you don't change soon, it will be too late. Listen carefully..."

Sheila and Mark opened their eyes simultaneously. Directly in front of Sheila's fifth-floor balcony was a large flying saucer, hovering, glowing bright yellow, and flashing what Mark interpreted as warning lights.

Kaplow!

The flying saucer disappeared before the buckshot could reach it.

"What the fuck?" Mark said, snapping out of his trance-like state, rushing to the balcony railing, and searching for the source of the gunshot blast.

Sheila was right beside him.

Mark saw a man with long, scraggly hair leaning over the edge of a balcony above them. He held a shotgun. "I saw what you did," the man said.

"What do you think you're doing, Garrett?" Sheila said. "You can't go firing off a shotgun in a residential neighborhood."

"Like fuck I can't," Garrett said, glaring down at them, the barrel of his gun poking over the balcony railing. "I saw what you did. I heard what you said. You're calling for aliens."

"They mean us no harm," Mark said, thinking that this situation had the potential to escalate rapidly out of control.

"Like fuck they do," Garrett said. "First the government said UFOs don't exist. And, if they do exist, the government said, then they mean to wipe out the human race. Your involvement makes you an accessory to murder. An accessory to genocide."

Sheila's face tightened. "Put that gun away before I call the cops."

Mark quickly grabbed her arm. He pulled her back from the edge of the balcony, whispering, "He's got a gun. He's off his rocker. You can't reason with a psycho."

But she shook him off, returning to the edge of the balcony and leaning up. Mark felt helpless but to follow her lead.

Garrett was still glaring at them. Now the barrel of his gun slid slowly side-to-side along the top of the steel balcony railing. It produced a terrifying metallic scraping sound.

"Garrett," Sheila said, noticeably more composed, her tone conciliatory. "Sorry for calling in the aliens. We won't do it again. I promise. Now would you put that gun away and go inside?"

Garrett grinned, exposing large gaps in his chiseled yellow teeth. "Can you say please?"

"Please," Sheila said.

"Please," Mark said. "We don't want anyone to get hurt."

"Okay," Garrett said. "But, trust me, the only ones who are gonna get hurt are those fucking alien bastards, the ones that wanna wipe out the human race."

Garrett lifted the barrel of his sawed-off shotgun, pointed it to the stars, and as Sheila and Mark both froze in fear, said, "Bang!"

Then he chuckled, grinned, pulled the gun out of sight, and said, "You guys have a good night, now. And don't go doing anything I wouldn't do."

A few minutes later, Mark and Sheila huddled together on the sofa sipping hot chocolate. They were silent for a long time, both thinking of next steps.

Finally, Mark said, "I really think we should call the cops. I mean, do you know that lunatic?"

"I kind of feel sorry for him," Sheila said. "He moved in about a year ago. He's been really neighborly to me up until this point. Helps me out with things sometimes. His mother and father died exactly six months apart. Then his wife left him and his two kids disowned him. Then friend after friend after friend abandoned him, and I'm not only talking on social media. You might've already guessed, but he's got a problem with drugs and alcohol."

"Frankly I think his problems run a lot deeper than that."

"I'm sure they do. But I'd be kind of afraid to call the cops on him. I have this gut feeling it would end up in a hostage-taking, a lengthy stand-off, long negotiations, and probably a few murders. Garrett Scott is a long way past the edge of his rope."

"Isn't that why we *should* call the cops?" Mark said.

"I dunno. I'm surprised no neighbors complained over that gunshot. Probably because it's Saturday and they're all partying."

"I saw a few lights go on. Maybe someone has already called the cops."

"Could be," Shelia said. "I'll let you decide if we should call the cops. I don't want this hanging over my head if we do nothing and someone ends up dying because of it."

Mark felt he was—they were—between a rock and a hard place. To do nothing might mean they'd have blood on their hands. To do something might mean they'd have blood on their hands. Damned if they do, damned if they don't.

"I don't know," Mark said. "I..."

He was interrupted by three loud knocks on the door.

They both practically jumped out of their skins.

Sheila rushed to the door and stopped behind it. The door wasn't equipped with the benefit of a peephole. "Who is it?"

As it turned out, she wouldn't need one this time.

"It's me, Sheila," Garrett said. "I'm sorry. I've come to make a peace offering."

Mark approached the door. "Are you sure you should open it?" he whispered.

Sheila looked at Mark and turned the deadbolt. "Maybe our problem has been solved for us. Let's talk to him. He's a troubled soul."

Before Mark could respond, she swung the door open.

Garrett stood there frowning, a beaten man. He had a six-pack of Budweiser in one hand, a sawed-off shotgun in the other.

Beginning to panic, Mark attempted to close the door but then stopped when Garrett started talking.

"You've gotta help me," Garrett said. "Jeanette, that nosy bitch next door, called the cops on me. She banged on my door and told me the cops are coming." He offered up the shotgun, stock side first, and Mark, without thinking, took it.

"Come on in," Sheila said. He entered and she closed the door quickly behind him, and locked it. She motioned him into the living room and he sat in an armchair in front of the couch.

Mark and Sheila sat on the opposite sofa next to their respective hot chocolates.

Mark carefully put the shotgun on the coffee table in front of them.

Garrett set the six-pack on an end table, extracted one, cracked it, and took a long pull. He finished, belched loudly, and said, "You guys want one?"

"Don't mind if I do," Mark said. He rose, grabbed two from the six-pack, handed one to Sheila, and sat down next to her.

They thanked Garrett and popped open their cans

"I know I shouldn't be shooting at fucking flying saucers," Garrett said. "I just got paranoid all of a sudden. You know, that's what politicians have been telling us for years. That aliens are a hostile force."

"That's because if we believe that then they can feed the industrial military complex," Mark said. "The war machine. To justifiably build up armaments, they need an enemy."

"Well, whatever," Garrett said. "I've been going through a lot of shit lately. Sorry I did that. And sorry I freaked out on you guys."

Sheila began pacing. "Wait a minute. We don't have time for this. The cops are coming. Right?"

Garrett nodded. "That's why I'm here. That shotgun. It's illegal. Can you guys hide it for me? Then I'll just go back upstairs and deny the whole thing when they arrive. No weapon, no proof. Right? As long as you guys don't rat me out?"

"We won't do that," Sheila said.

"They can't search your premises without a warrant," Mark said.

"It's too late for that," Sheila said, carrying the shotgun into the bedroom.

While she was gone, Garrett sized Mark up. "Are you her new boyfriend?"

"No. A friend and a colleague. We work together. I'm Mark, by the way."

"Garrett, but I guess you already know that."

Mark nodded.

Sheila returned, looking stressed.

"Garrett," she said. "I think you should go back to your apartment now. If the cops arrive and you're not home, it's probably gonna look worse."

Four loud knocks on the door.

"Who is it?" Sheila said.

"It's the police."

"Oh shit," Garrett said. "They're here."

As Sheila approached the door, suddenly all three of them were blinded by a bright beam of light that cascaded into the apartment from the open sliding-glass balcony door. The beam enveloped Garrett and lifted him off the floor.

He dropped his beer, blood-shot eyes widening with fear, and said, "Shit, karma's a bitch, ain't it?"

In a lightning-swift motion, he was sucked out of the apartment.

Mark and Sheila rushed out to the balcony and watched his body, guided by the laser-like beam, float into a glowing yellow flying saucer. Then the UFO disappeared.

More loud knocks at the door. From outside the door, "I said it's the police. Open up."

Sheila rushed to the door.

Mark collected the beer cans, put them in the kitchen, returned, and approached the door as Sheila opened it.

Two cops—one obese, one thin—stood at the entrance, the thin cop gripping his holstered weapon.

"I'm Officer Colin Mason and my partner is Officer Rick Jefferies," the obese cop said.

"Sheila Samuelson and Mark Waters," Sheila said.

Officer Colin Mason nodded. "Sorry to disturb you, but your neighbor upstairs called us. She claims to have seen and heard a Garrett Scott—her next-door neighbor—fire a shotgun at a... well, a UFO, is what she said. Did you folks see anything?"

Sheila rolled her eyes and grinned, an Oscar-winning performance. "No, I haven't." She turned to Mark. "Have you?"

"No."

"Did the complaint come from Jeanette Flaherty?" Sheila asked.

"Yes, as a matter of fact, it did," Colin said.

Sheila rolled her eyes again. "Jeanette, as you may have gathered, is not all there. If you talk to her long enough, you'll find out she's seen a lot of other strange things besides UFOs."

"I kind of gathered that," Colin said. "The man above you, Garrett Scott, doesn't appear to be home. Do you know him?"

"Yes," Sheila said. "He's been a helpful neighbor."

"Do you know where he is?" Colin asked.

"No," Sheila said. "Why would I know where he is?"

Rick scratched his chin, seeing his partner was becoming flustered. "Jeanette claims she saw Garrett enter your apartment with a shotgun. Is he here?"

"No one here but us," Sheila said. "Feel free to look around."

"That won't be necessary," Colin said. "Sorry to have bothered you."

The officers started to leave.

As Sheila was about to close the door, Jeanette appeared in the hallway. She was a thin elderly woman wearing a pink polka dot nightgown and white slippers. Her thinning gray hair stuck out in several directions. It looked as if she'd just stuck her finger in an electrical outlet. She swung her arms wildly as she approached the officers, her eyes wild.

"The aliens abducted him," Jeanette said. "I saw it with my own eyes. The alien laser beam sucked Garrett right out of her apartment and right into their spaceship. The aliens got him, I tell you. The aliens got him. He's been abducted."

"We'll look into that, Miss Flaherty," Colin said, rolling his eyes and heading toward the elevator. "But right now we have better things to do."

***

The following Saturday evening, Mark waited anxiously for Sheila to arrive, pacing back and forth in his living room. They'd picked his quiet house on a quaint tree-lined street to conduct their next alien contact mission. He owned a house at the end of a cul-de-sac. His backyard backed onto a large field that was bordered by woods. They'd both agreed it would make an ideal setting to reconnect with extraterrestrials.

Before he'd left Sheila's a week ago, they'd sworn each other to secrecy. The masses had been fed a steady diet of bullshit for the last umpteen years regarding the existence of UFOs anyway, so they were unlikely to bring a lot of believers on board. If anything, they'd only be jeopardizing their sane reputations, perhaps even their careers.

They had both vowed to continue their research on UFOs and read everything they could find from what they viewed to be credible sources.

Mark was anxious and apprehensive for many reasons. One, Sheila had told him that Colin and Rick, the investigating officers, had returned to her apartment on Wednesday after Garrett's long-lost uncle had filed a missing persons report on his nephew. Of course, Sheila hadn't invited them into the unit. After all, she was still concealing the illegal firearm and denying any knowledge of the whereabouts of Garrett.

Two, the cops were getting a little more suspicious. Especially after Sheila was unwilling to let them search her apartment. According to Sheila, the Colin cop had even threatened to return with a search warrant. *He was probably bluffing*, Mark thought, but they couldn't take any chances. For this mission, Sheila would bring the shotgun, which they'd agreed to bury in the field behind Mark's house. Bury the hatchet—or shotgun as it were—once and for all.

And three, Sheila had told Mark that she had a surprise for him. Although they'd been friends for many years and had even cried on each other's shoulders when they'd suffered mutual, but unconnected break-up-heartbreak with their respective spouses, Mark had never really considered Sheila girlfriend material. But they did have a lot in common. And if he really analyzed his feelings, he would have to admit that there was a seed of attraction for Sheila that had taken root and begun to sprout.

What was this surprise? Was she gonna confess her feelings for him? Were they gonna then fall in love and live happily ever after? Or, did the surprise have nothing to do with a confession of love? Would all his built-up hopes and expectations be shattered like a glass menagerie?

And four, and lastly, there was the whole question of tampering with advanced civilizations. The ETs had already abducted Garrett.

Are we next? Mark didn't think he was ready for a life on Mars quite yet.

Before he could ponder that question, he looked out the window and saw Sheila's car pull into his driveway at 8:00 pm precisely, their agreed-upon time.

After they got comfortably settled on the sofa in his candle-lit living room—exchanging a few social pleasantries and small talk—Mark couldn't help but notice that Sheila had gone to a lot of fuss with her appearance. Normally a plain-Jane sort of woman, she had curled her mid-length auburn hair and decorated her face with eye shadow, lipstick, and a fetchingly pink shade of blush. Generally a jeans and T-shirt kind of woman, she wore a pair of form-fitting black slacks and a tight red V-neck blouse, the neckline dotted with tiny tantalizing black roses. She also wore a gold necklace with a shiny gold heart. And her scent. Lilacs and honey. Incredibly alluring. Incredibly appetizing.

This in contrast to Mark's worn blue jeans, tattered blue sweatshirt, and slightly disheveled short black hair. He had missed the dress code cue evidently, but, heck, they would soon be burying a shotgun in the woods. That certainly wasn't a black-tie affair.

"Wow," Mark said over a glass of white wine. "You look... stunning."

Even behind the blush, Mark noticed the blush.

"Thanks," Sheila said. "It's part of my surprise."

Mark felt his heart flutter. "I should've dressed a little better. But, you know, I'm not used to this with you." *Insert foot in mouth.*

"Never mind. You look great. At least you shaved and showered. I can smell the Irish Spring. I love that smell."

Sheila pointed to the beige knapsack, containing the shotgun, on the coffee table. "Besides, we still gotta bury this. You're dressed to do the digging. I'll supervise."

She moved a little closer to him and Mark felt butterflies tickling the lining of his stomach.

"Fair enough," Mark said. "I'm dying to know. What's the surprise?"

She sipped her wine, set the glass down, and looked Mark square in the eyes. She looked apprehensive and excited at the same time. "It's about the extraterrestrials..."

Mark's heart sank.

"I mean, I think, if we can, we should leave here," Sheila said.

"You mean go live on Mars or something?"

"Where ever their civilization is. You heard the prophetic voice last Saturday. You remember what he said: 'You recklessly destroy your planet and yourselves. If you don't change soon, it will be too late.'"

"I know," Mark said, beginning to feel hopeful. *Wait a minute. She just said she wanted to go live on another planet. With me.* "I agree with what he said."

You've read stuff by Paul Hellyer, haven't you?" Sheila asked.

Mark was very familiar with Hellyer. A former Canadian Minister of Defense, he'd been interviewed several times about his knowledge of extraterrestrials. He'd written a number of books on ETs and the state of our world. Hellyer firmly believed that humankind was hell-bent on its own destruction if it didn't change soon. The warring nature of humans, fossil fuels, climate change, and even our monetary system, according to Hellyer, was all messed up.

Mark nodded. "I reread some of it last week. I know he thinks we're going to hell in a handbasket. I think he's right."

"Well," Sheila said, "what do you think?"

"About Hellyer?"

"No, about us leaving Earth forever."

"I don't know. Do you really think it's as easy as we decide to fly off into the sunset together and it just happens?"

"Something like that. I mean, look, they took Garrett. And *we've* made contact. They want us. We've been chosen. I believe that from the bottom of my heart."

"Well, for one, they probably view Garrett as an enemy. Maybe they're gonna reform him or something."

"Who knows? But think about it. I mean, when I really think about it, I lost faith in humanity a long time ago. We as a people aren't gonna change our materialistic nature. We're not gonna change our greed or corruption. We're not gonna change our hostility toward our neighbors. Racism, and on and on it goes. We're gonna keep on killing people. Keep on killing the planet. Hellyer wrote his survival guide for the human species back in 2010 and that's over ten years ago now. Has anything really changed since then?"

"Not really," Mark admitted. He wanted to steer the conversation to their potential role together in this new civilization, never mind if they'd get accepted. But he could see Sheila was very passionate about this topic and needed to get some things off her chest.

"No, it hasn't," Sheila continued. "If anything, it's gotten worse. Like you told Garrett last Saturday. The government wants us to fear aliens so they can use that fear to manipulate us. It's the big lie, the big cover-up, so they can feed the big hungry war machine monster. First, it was the communists. Then it was the terrorists. Now it's the extraterrestrials. We... they... need an enemy to keep the industrial military complex alive and thriving. To make us think that we need them for defense and whatever else. Well, I'm tired of it. Aren't you?"

"In a way, I am. But I thought I still had a few more things to do on this planet before moving to another one."

"Like what?"

"Well, for starters, it would be nice to have a girlfriend..." *Oh, shit. Was that a Freudian slip?*

Sheila leaned over, wrapped her arms around him, and planted a long, wet, passionate kiss on his lips.

Tingly sensations shot through Mark's body. That decided it. He'd follow Sheila to hell and back to win her love—or to Mars and not back, if he had to.

She released him, gazed into his eyes, and smiled. "I guess I should've told you that part of the surprise in the beginning. I want you with me on this new journey... because I think I love you."

"I think I love you too, Sheila. I think I've been thinking that for some time actually."

"Me too," she said, hugging and kissing him again. "Do you think I'll do as a girlfriend?"

"I think so," Mark said.

"You think so?"

"I know so."

"That's a lot of thinks."

"I know."

Mark grabbed the knapsack. "We better get cracking, honey. We've got a shotgun to bury and some aliens to talk to."

***

About an hour later, the shotgun safely buried in the forest, they sat beside each other cross-legged on a small grassy knoll. They were in the middle of the field, surrounded by the forest. Mark thought it was a picture-perfect evening for contacting aliens. Dead calm. Not even a gentle breeze. The crescent moon shone brightly and the night sky was awash in a spellbinding array of twinkling stars.

He took Sheila's hand. "Are you sure you're ready for this?"

She nodded, gazing lovingly into his eyes.

"What about our families and friends?" Mark said. "If we leave, how will we say goodbye? I mean, I've only got Mom and Dad and a handful of friends. But you, your mother and father, two brothers and two sisters, and you're close to all of them. Not to mention all the friends you have scattered around the globe."

"Don't worry," Sheila said confidently. "I'm sure the ETs will show us how to say goodbye."

"I'll have to trust you on that one."

"You'll have to trust me on that one."

"Hey, I just thought of something. If we're leaving anyway, we didn't even have to bother hiding the shotgun."

"We don't know for sure we're leaving."

"Right."

They closed their eyes and began meditating. After a while, they brought themselves to a deeper state of consciousness. In their respective minds, they began calling the ETs, revising their thoughts to indicate a willingness to leave Earth forever and join in an effort to save humankind from its own destruction. For a long time, nothing happened.

Then Sheila opened her eyes. "I felt something. Did you?"

"Yeah, it was that powerful warmth I felt before, but this time only fleeting."

"Same for me."

"Let's keep our eyes open, look to the stars, and will ET to come."

"Okay."

For a long time nothing happened. And, just when they were ready to give up, they saw it. A glowing yellow flying saucer descended from the heavens, swooped down with lightning speed, circled the tree-lined perimeter of the field, and then vanished.

"Wow," Mark said. "Incredible."

"We're not alone. We never were."

They waited silently for about another half hour, but nothing reappeared, and no sensations permeated their bodies.

Mark was getting impatient. "Maybe we're not ready."

"What's that?" Sheila said, pointing toward Mark's house.

Mark turned and saw two small white lights—flashlights—in the distance, bobbing and weaving. Maybe three hundred feet away, coming toward them. Then he heard the unmistakable voice of Officer Colin Mason in the distance and clear as a bell.

"I just wanna ask them some questions. Garrett's been gone for a week now. And he was last seen entering Sheila's apartment with a shotgun. Don't you think that paints a pretty grim picture?"

"I think we're barking up the wrong tree," Officer Rick Jefferies said. "I don't believe a word of what that Jeanette says. She's probably got a weekend pass from a nuthouse."

"Whatever," Colin said. "We gotta follow every lead."

"Shit. What do we do?" Mark whispered. "This doesn't look good."

But Sheila wasn't whispering. "We tell them the truth."

"What?" Mark whispered. "That aliens abducted Garrett and we buried the shotgun because we knew the cops wouldn't buy it?"

"Something like that?"

Now less than fifty feet away, Colin called out to them: "Excuse me, are you guys Mark Waters and Sheila Samuelson?"

"Look," Sheila said, pointing to the sky.

All bodies froze as the blinding light of the flying saucer descended upon them. It flew directly above Sheila and Mark, hovered for a split second, and then a long white beam shot down and encompassed them.

Mark felt his body begin to levitate. He grabbed Sheila's hand and looked into her eyes.

She smiled, calm, serene, and confident. "It's time."

"Sorry guys," Mark said turning to the officers. "This is gonna have to wait."

***

"Holy shit," Colin said after the UFO had sucked Sheila and Mark inside of it and disappeared in a flash. "How the fuck do we file a report on this one?"

"Fuck the report," Rick said. "I need a goddamned drink."

***

Mark opened his eyes, sat up, and looked around. Sheila was lying beside him on something remotely resembling an ambulance stretcher, her chest rising and falling in a steady and even rhythm.

He sighed, surveying his surroundings. They were in a huge, circular, shiny metal room. It was dotted with many round windows, black with shiny white dots. To his right, there was a wall of tiny flashing green and red lights, laser-like yellow graphs zigzagging spasmodically, and brightly illuminated digital maps of a complex galaxy. A complicated operating system of sorts. He heard a steady but not displeasing humming sound. Above him was a rectangular-shaped metal object suspended in mid-air, also with a series of flashing lights and zigzagging graphs. He scanned every nook and cranny. Not a soul in sight.

"Sheila," he said, sliding off the single bed of sorts and touching her arm.

She slowly opened her eyes. "We're here. We made it."

Mark helped her to her feet. "Yes, we did."

She hugged him warmly and kissed him softly on the lips. "Our new life."

"Evidently so."

They locked hands, walked over to one of the windows, and peered out.

Below them, Mark recognized planet Earth. It was shrinking as the spacecraft sped away from it.

"Look," Mark said. "Earth. Take a good look, it might be the last time we see it."

Sheila leaned in, pressing her head to the window. "Wow. It looks beautiful."

Then a small fiery explosion ignited on planet Earth.

"Look," Sheila said. "It looks like a bomb blast."

"Shit," Mark said. "Maybe we're too late to save humankind."

They watched the explosion rise, mushroom into the sky, slowly shrink, and then begin to fade.

"I wonder where that is?" Sheila said.

"That's North Korea," a small voice from behind them said.

They spun around and saw a diminutive glowing white man with a smooth body, elongated head, large luminescent green eyes, and small dots for a nose and mouth.

"Actually, that *was* North Korea," the extraterrestrial said. "It's gone now. Obliterated by a nuclear bomb. And if we don't act fast, the United States and Canada will be next."

Something in the Woods

"There's something in the woods," Marg Davenport said, her voice tinged with panic. "I saw it. I heard it." Wearing a long floral-patterned pink nightgown, her bulky, middle-aged frame was silhouetted by the incoming moon's rays as she knelt on a chair by the window and peered through the Venetian blinds into the blackened forest. She had gotten up a few minutes earlier to relieve herself and had returned to bed. She'd settled in next to her snoring husband, pulled the blankets up over her head, and then had been roused from her repose by a horrifyingly loud roar coming from the woods, followed by the snapping of twigs, a mere thirty feet away from her bedroom. Rushing to the window, she was sure she'd seen a large black shadow leap onto her lawn-covered clearing for an instant before spinning around and vanishing back inside the dense woods.

She looked at her husband, trumpeting a full-throttled musical rhapsody through his mouth and nostrils. "Did you hear me, Thorvald?"

He stirred and stopped snoring. "What?"

"There's something in the woods. I saw it. I heard it."

"Of course, there's something in the woods. We live in the country, remember? It's full of wild animals."

"This wasn't a coyote or a fox," Marg insisted. "It was much bigger than that. The size of the Sasquatch."

Thor rolled over and, through blinking and sleep-saturated eyes, looked at the digital alarm clock. "Come on, Marg. It's three-thirty in the morning. You know I gotta work tomorrow. Can we discuss this another time? Please?"

With trembling hands, Marg closed the blinds and returned to bed. "Okay." She kissed her husband on the cheek. "Sorry. You're right. Get some sleep."

Thor grunted and rolled over and gave her his back.

As she lay there staring at the dark ceiling, a multitude of dark images flashed through her mind. She reasoned her mental muscle was trying to identify the intruder and wrap a layer of sense around something that seemed to defy logic. Thor began a nasally snore, a resumption of his earlier rhapsody. Ten years ago, the snoring would've driven her over a cliff, but now it was music to her ears. His snoring, a sleep apnea condition, slowly extricated the shadowy demons and began lulling her back to sleep. She felt consciousness ceding to sub-consciousness, that mysterious and magical plane of existence where almost everything seemed to defy reason and rationality. As the last vestiges of wakeful cognizance slowly melted away, she vowed to examine the forest the following day in an effort to frame the sighting in a way that would make sense to Thor, who was cynical and skeptical by nature.

***

While Thor was away pounding nails at his construction job, Marg, a stay-at-home housewife, pushed her way through rustling dead leaves and snapping twigs and searched the forest for signs of a monster. On a whim, she'd armed herself with a hammer, a bottle of water, and a flashlight, even though it was a clear and sunny fall afternoon on Prince Edward Island, where the couple shared a home on twenty acres of God's green woods.

She arrived at a spot where she thought the monster had appeared and studied the ground around her. Twigs. Moss. Fallen orange, red, and yellow leaves. Saplings. Browning, tall grass. Dying ferns. Other indigenous plants of the forest going through the life cycle of the changing seasons, but no signs of a recent ground disturbance.

Another ten minutes of poking around proved fruitless. She was already well into the thick forest. Other than a chattering squirrel, seemingly squawking at her invasion of its otherwise peaceful presence in Mother Nature's paradise, she could find nothing out of the ordinary. She sighed heavily and turned around, intent on erasing it from her mind and settling into her rocker with a good book and a hot cup of tea after finishing the household chores and planning Thor's dinner. She started her journey home.

Snap!

The sound startled her and she raised the hammer high in the air, realizing for the first timed how tightly strung she was. "Who's there?"

Other than the annoying squawk of a circling blue jay, also evidently taking exception to her presence, she was met by silence. She made her way over to the area where the snap had originated and arched an eyebrow at the sight. A large spruce tree, about twenty-two inches wide and a good fifty feet tall, had come down in the forest, ripped from its rotting tree trunk about eight feet up its trunk.

That's normal, she said to herself. *Dead trees fall in the forest all the time.* But as she considered the ground around it, she stopped at a spot that made her jaw drop and shivers creep up her spine. It was a footprint, almost two feet long. She felt her heart rate quicken and contemplated bolting but remained nailed to the spot, choosing instead to inspect the downed tree trunk, only a few feet from where the footprint was. Three-quarters of the way up the tree trunk, her eyes stopped at what resembled a claw print. The monster or whatever it was had evidently struck the tree with such devastating force it had peeled away some of the bark and left its malicious mark.

"What? Monsters pushing down trees in the forest? What the hell's going on?" Marg suddenly realized she'd spoken aloud. The sound of her own voice sounded eerily unfamiliar. Without thinking twice, she got her feet moving, tucked the hammer in her apron pocket, and flew out of the forest. By the time she reached the comfort of her back porch, she was breathing heavily and her forehead gleamed with a slick coat of perspiration.

Slowly, her brain began to process the information. "Damn," she said, realizing she'd forgotten to bring her cellphone and knowing there'd be little chance Thor would believe her or even be willing to visit the spot without proof. And by the time he arrived home from a long day of hard work, the sun would already be disappearing beyond the tall trees. From what she'd already experienced, she figured nighttime would be a bad time to return to the monster's site of destruction. Maybe tea would help calm her nerves and replenish her courage reserves for another intelligence-gathering return trip.

After a nerve-calming hot herbal tea, she spent an hour doing domestic chores. Then she started dinner, a spicy minestrone soup and one of Thor's favorites. After setting the culinary creation to simmer, she headed outside with her cellphone. Already a bank of clouds was starting to roll in and she hesitated on her lawn before entering the forest, wondering if the clouds were a bad omen. After a minute or so of contemplation, she dismissed the notion and plunged into the woods.

As best she could, she traced her old tracks and soon found herself at the place where she thought the fallen tree was. But it was gone. The area was surrounded by untrammeled moss and dead leaves, tall and healthy pine, spruce, oak, balsam fir, and maple trees. She silently cursed herself for not bringing bright pink marking tape the first time, or the second time for that matter, and marking not only the location but a pathway out.

Snaaaaaaaaaaaap!

She started at the sound but the tea-fueled courage reserves propelled her toward it. When she reached it, she was amazed and fearful at what she saw. It was the sight of the original downed tree all right. But the trunk had been freshly sheared off about three feet up, well below the claw marks. Most of the dead tree was lying in the forest, but the section in the middle was mysteriously missing. As well, the spot where the footprint was had been freshly camouflaged with twigs and dead leaves. It appeared as if someone or something was trying to cover their tracks.

She reached for her phone to photograph it anyway. Something was better than nothing. As she set the camera mode, the sound of thunderously retreating footsteps drove a wedge of fear into the pit of her stomach and she dropped her phone. She kneeled down to pick it up, but then froze, wondering if the footsteps would turn around and attack her. But they kept retreating rapidly and the sound eventually faded into nothingness. Taking deep breaths and close to full-blown panic, she picked up the phone, quickly snapped off six photos of the tree and surrounding area, and beat a hasty retreat the hell out of there.

Halfway out, thunder erupted and heavy rain began sheeting down on her. By the time she arrived home, she was drenched and shivering. She took a hot shower, changed her clothes, and drank another tea before she was calm enough to begin to process exactly what had happened.

Something strange is going on around here. And I aim to find out what it is.

***

Thor plucked a morsel of minestrone soup from his thick beard, contemplated eating it, and then changed his mind and placed it on a napkin next to his empty bowl. He wiped a hand through his thick mop of gray-brown hair and looked at his wife with a wide grin. "That was delicious, honey. You've done it again."

"Thanks."

After Thor had arrived home, Marg's first impulse was to tell him about the monster's wrath. But four things had changed her mind. One. He'd arrived home well past sunset and it was too dark to show him anything. Two. It was still raining buckets. Three. She had very little evidence. He would quickly explain away the downed tree as a natural occurrence. The missing section of the tree trunk? Well, for all she knew the monster would try and undermine her efforts again and replace it by the time they returned. Four. It took a lot of evidence to convince a Doubting Thomas.

"Did you find your monster?" Thor asked with a wry grin.

She sighed heavily. "Just a downed tree in the forest."

"Trees fall in the forest."

"I know. If I find any evidence, I'll let you know."

"Please do," he said, unable to disguise his sarcastic tone. Who knew if he'd even tried? "I wanna be the first to know if we're getting invaded by monsters."

Marg tucked an errant strand of graying hair behind her ear and frowned. "Oh, be quiet already," she said, unable to conceal her growing agitation. "If I found a two-foot long footprint beside the tree and a monster-sized claw mark eight feet up of what's left of it, you probably still wouldn't believe me."

Thor stood. "Maybe I would. And maybe I wouldn't. But I would like to know where that downed tree is. We could use some more firewood for the winter."

"I'll show you tomorrow," she said, starting to feel a sense of renewed hope. *He needs to get the crap scared out of him. Then he'll believe.*

He pecked her on the cheek and started out of the room. He turned around in the doorway. "Sounds good. We're changing jobsites tomorrow and I'll be off early. Supposed to be sunny as well."

"Sounds good," Marg said, deciding to play his game. "You'll be shocked when you see the monster-sized footprint and claw mark."

A look of belief tinted his dark eyes for a split second. Then he squinted and grinned. "Pardon my language, my dear, but now I know you're fucking with me."

"You'll find out tomorrow," she said as he left the room.

As she hand-washed the dishes, a plan began to jell. After Thor left for work, she would retrace her steps, clearly mark the path with marking tape and manufacture a claw mark and a footprint. She liked the idea, not least of all because it would wreak a modicum of havoc on her husband for his cynical and doubting ways. Revenge. After all, it hadn't been the first ghost or monster story she'd ever told him. There'd been a few others before that, all of them met with that same smirking cynicism.

Recalling a famous quote from former US President Harry S. Truman, her frown slowly morphed into a smile. "If you can't convince them, confuse them."

"What's that, honey?" Thor asked over the drone of the television.

"Nothing, my dear. Nothing at all."

***

Armed with a claw hammer, an oversized boot she'd scored from a local thrift store, her cellphone, and a roll of pink marking tape, Marg set off the following afternoon in search of a little trickery and deception. Well, if she had to be totally honest with herself, it wasn't completely trickery and deception. She'd seen the monster, heard the growls, heard the retreating footfalls, and witnessed the footprint and the claw print. Problem was, none of the evidence still existed. So, she would just have to bend the rules a little to convince that skeptical bastard.

With twigs snapping underfoot, she weaved through the forest, marking her way to where she thought the devastation had occurred. But once again the forest confused her and she got lost and disoriented for a few minutes before backtracking and finding the right trajectory. Finally, under cloudy skies and an intensifying chilly wind (so much for the weatherman's nice-day forecast), she arrived at the monster site.

It was just how she'd left it yesterday. She walked the perimeter, in search of the missing section of the tree. Nothing.

Undeterred, she used the hammer to rake claw marks in the tree trunk and the boot to plant an oversized footprint on the ground. After she pushed the boot around in the moss for a while, she grabbed a twig and drew lines that extended from the toe, creating the appearance of massive claw marks. She whistled as she worked, pleased with her efforts, excited at the possibility of messing with her husband. Teach him a lesson. Confuse him. Maybe even scare the crap out of him.

Fidgeting with her hands an hour later in the comfort of her home, she waited with nervous anticipation for Thor to arrive. Finally, she saw his pickup roll up the driveway at three-thirty in the afternoon.

She ran out to greet him as he exited the truck. "How did your day go, hon?'

"Fine, just fine. And your monster quest?"

"I have the spot marked. Wanna go now?"

Thor winked and grinned. "Don't you think it would be more exciting if we went at dusk? You know, provide that element of fear?"

Why not? Better chance of scaring him that way. But yet she hesitated before responding. "Are you sure?"

"Sure I'm sure. I'll have some of that delicious minestrone soup of yours, catch a shower and some news, and then we'll head out. If you have it marked, I'll bring the chainsaw tomorrow and buck it up for firewood."

Time seemed to drag on as Marg waited for the witching hour. When she saw the last orange and pink remnants of the setting sun disappear beyond the tree line, she said, "I think now's a good time."

Thor grinned. "Let's give it another half hour. I want the perfect atmosphere."

To her disappointment, it was approaching six in the evening by the time she was able to drag her husband out the door. It seemed as if her little plan was beginning to backfire while he'd relished in tormenting her. And thanks to an unexpected thick bank of clouds and a surprise forecast calling for PEI's first snowfall to arrive that evening, the night was almost pitch-black by the time they entered the woods.

Marg trained her flashlight beam in front of her, shivering from a mixture of fear and plunging temperatures.

"I hope you're not doing this to scare me," he said, his crunching footfalls following hers.

"I did see the claw mark on the tree. Saw the footprint in the forest. I really did. And I heard the retreating footsteps, and that horrific growl the first time I saw him."

"Sure you did, honey. Sure you did. Let's just get this over with."

Marg felt her neck muscles stiffen. "Damn you, Thor. Why can't you believe anything I tell you?"

"That's a sweeping generalization, honey. I believe most of what you tell me. Just not as it relates to the supernatural. And don't take it personally. I don't believe what anyone says about ghosts and monsters. I just don't believe. And I never will, unless I see proof. Period."

His attitude was bringing her to the boiling point. They were halfway to the site and, over their heated discussion, Marg heard other sounds. Snapping twigs nearby. The hooting of an owl. The chattering of a squirrel. And some mysterious hissing white noise she couldn't identify. Due to Thor's attitude, she tried to ignore the sounds, knowing that to mention them would be to bring on more of his ridicule.

Thor was still blathering something about a rational explanation for everything when Marg stopped, about twenty feet in front of the last tape mark. Out of the corner of her eye, she thought she saw a large and looming shadow emerge briefly before vanishing. But how could she see a shadow in the black of the night? Illuminated by her flashlight beam perhaps? She decided not to bother mentioning it.

Thor bumped into her. "Sorry, hon. I didn't realize you stopped."

"Never mind. It's straight ahead." She pointed her flashlight, circling the tree stump with its beam. Fear and panic started to seize her. "You go first."

"Are you getting scared?"

"Just shut up and go. I'll wait here for the all-clear."

Wordlessly, Thor stepped in front of her, crunching his way forward. He stopped at the tree trunk. "Oh my fucking God!"

"Don't you play games with me, Thorvald!"

"I'm not... I'm not playing games. Come take a look at this." His voice was hoarse with rising panic.

Marg knew him well enough to distinguish between his cynically mocking tone and his petrified voice. She hadn't seen her husband scared that often, but two years ago while he was bucking up storm-downed trees in the forest, he'd slipped and the chain dipped and ripped a long gash down the inside of his thigh before he'd even realized what'd happened. He'd managed to tourniquet the wound and practically crawl out of the forest. By the time he'd arrived home, he'd lost a hell of a lot of blood and, in a horrified tone, had said, "I don't wanna die, honey. Please help me. Please help me." She'd rushed him to the hospital where doctors later told her that, had she been five minutes later, her husband would've bled to death. The wound had required sixty-seven stitches and three quarts of transfused blood.

Marg dipped into dwindling courage reserves and slowly moved to where her husband stood. When she reached him, she realized his face had turned chalk-white, his eyes were bugged out, and his mouth hung wide open.

He pointed. "Over there."

Marg trained the flashlight beam to where Thor's was and her mouth dropped open. Even through a few snowflakes that had begun drifting lazily down, she saw several large footprints forming a circle. She traced the footsteps to the middle of the circle. Something reflected off the flashlight beam and momentarily blinded her.

"You see that?" Thor said.

"The footsteps?" she said, covering her eyes. "Of course."

"Not only that. The middle of the circle. Look."

Against her better judgment, she moved toward the center of the circle, realizing grimly, as she approached, that what had blinded her was a reflection from something wet. Blood. Little droplets of blood were splattered among the footprints. A puddle of blood was in the middle of the circle. And bloody animal entrails: intestines, tufts of matted fur, a fang, and what appeared to be a—*no, it can't be*—a beating heart.

She retreated quickly, nearly slipping on ground that was rapidly being coated by falling snow. She felt a firm grip on her arm, and looked at her husband, still wide-eyed and horrified, trying to speak.

But the words wouldn't quite come. "Le... le... let's..."

"GO!" Marg shouted. The command was followed by a giddy and clipped scream that Marg vaguely understood had come from her own mouth. She was on the verge of panic.

She tugged on his arm, hauling him out of the forest. He followed obediently and for the most part silently—but for the rasping sounds of panicked breathing.

"Grrrrrr... grrrrr... grrrrrrrr!!!"

They stopped dead in their tracks.

"Thor," Marg said, gripping his shoulders with both hands and shaking him. "Come back to me. I need you right now. That sound. It's ahead of us. What do we do?"

"Le... le... let's..."

She stopped shaking him and spoke directly into his ear. "Thor, not now. Please!"

"Grrrrrr... grrrrr... grrrrrrrr!!!

"Aaaaaaaaaaahhh!" The scream came from Marg's mouth, and now she felt Thor's firm grip on her wrist.

"I... I'm back," he said, stepping in front of her with the flashlight and veering to the left. "Follow me. We'll take another route. I know this spot."

Thankful she was for her husband to take the lead. She was so terrified she thought she too would lose the ability to speak, function, and think rationally.

They were moving quickly now, snapping twigs underfoot. Thor patiently held his wife's hand, guiding her safely around looming trees and dangerously overhanging branches. As they got closer, Marg saw the light at the end of the terrifying tunnel. The light that illuminated their back porch. The light of salvation and safety.

If there was a time to pray, although she'd never thought much of religion, she knew it was now. *Please God, get us out of this mess, I pray to you. Get us home safely, I beg you. Please God, don't abandon us in our time of need. Help us now and I'll be your devotee forever.* "Amen."

"Are you praying, Marg?"

"Yeah. You got a problem with that?"

"No."

As they reached the clearing surrounding their house, they heard the ferocious growl of the beast again, but this time much fainter.

But it was enough to send them sprinting for their back door. Thor released her hand and said, "Run as fast as you can."

Thor scrambled onto the porch first, pushed the door open, and stepped aside as Marg stumbled into the house, dropping her flashlight on the floor, steadying herself on a wall, and then plopping into the warm comfort of a sofa next to a blazing wood stove.

Thor closed and locked the door, kicked off his boots, and plopped down next to her, straining to catch his breath.

Three minutes passed before their breathing returned to normal and they were able to talk.

Marg decided not to rub it in, although she couldn't resist the initial jab. "Now do you believe me?"

Thor nodded, the color slowly returning to his rugged face. "There's something in the woods, all right. And I aim to find out what it is."

***

For three days they'd been practically shut in. Temperatures had dipped to daytime highs of minus 5, and nighttime lows of minus 11 degrees Celsius. Hardly balmy conditions. And the snow hadn't let up. There was at least a foot of it outside and Thor's outdoor construction jobs had been delayed due to frigid temperatures, high winds, and persistent snow squalls. He'd tried to busy himself with snowplowing and tinkering around in one of the outbuildings, but Marg couldn't help noticing a little testiness that had pervaded his usual jocular demeanor.

They'd discussed the monster and what to do about it, Marg over a glass of wine, and Thor over more than a couple of strong shots of whiskey. Initially, Thor had tried to explain it away rationally, yet the size of the footprints—about two feet—defied all logical explanations. And the blood-curdling growls. Nothing like any animal they'd ever heard before. His next tact had been to swear Marg to silence, since he didn't want it spreading around the close-knit community that they thought their property was being invaded by a monster. "Sure as shit," to use Thor's words, "everyone will think we're fucking loony-tunes."

Neither of them had ventured back into the forest. Besides, the heavy snow probably would've hidden all traces of the monster. They'd paid special attention to tracks around their property but didn't see anything out of the ordinary: fox, raccoon, skunk, squirrel, coyote, and bird tracks. However, unanswered questions still lingered. What were they dealing with? What animal had it killed? Had the monster disappeared? Would it return? And if it did, were they next on its hit list?

Marg suspected all of these unanswered questions were contributing to her husband's irritability, as they were contributing to her own unease and growing anxiety. She'd also noticed that Thor hadn't been sleeping as well as he normally would. Three times she'd woken up in the middle of the night only to find him gazing out the bedroom window at the frozen wasteland, once shining a flashlight methodically back and forth across their snow-covered lawn.

Since that life-changing and ill-fated evening, they'd rarely discussed the monster.

Dishing up a portion of mashed potatoes, corn, and boneless beef short ribs to her husband, Marg then served herself and sat across from Thor. Between forkfuls of potatoes, she studied her him. His grizzled, weather-worn face seemed to have aged and dark circles leant a sinister edge to his coffee-brown eyes. His beard, normally trimmed daily, poked out at indifferent angles along with his hair; personal hygiene had evidently taken a backseat to his preoccupation with the monster.

Marg disinterestedly began poking at her corn. She looked out the window. More blowing snow. More frigid temperatures. The orange setting sun dipping in the distance and not even six in the evening. The atmosphere inside and outside was becoming more and more untenable and she was becoming concerned that if they carried on like this for much longer Thor's testiness would turn to nastiness. His behavior was already starting to get on her nerves and more than once she'd bitten her tongue to avoid saying something that might provoke an argument.

No. Enough was enough. "Thorvald?"

He didn't look up from his plate. He didn't have to. His eyes were on her, probing and penetrating. "What?!"

And the tone, far from friendly. Gone was the cheerful, *"What, honey?"*

"Either you're gonna have to accept what happened as a real-life encounter with a monster or you're gonna have to dismiss it out of hand and join the living again."

His eyes narrowed. He dropped his fork and it clattered onto his dinner plate. "What's that supposed to mean?"

"I mean, look at you. You haven't showered in three days. You're not sleeping. You don't trim your beard or comb your hair anymore. You're always looking out the window, wide-eyed, as if something's coming to get you. Before I wanted you to believe me, but now I don't care. I just want the old Thor back."

A shadow of the old softness returned to his eyes. "You know me, Marg, I just don't like things that I can't explain. I've never believed in anything like that." He squinted and a half dozen thin white lines pressed across his forehead. "Now this fucking monster thing has to show up and reduce all my beliefs to rubbish. And I can't even go into the forest to try and prove otherwise because of all this snow and fucking cold."

"You can always accept it and forget about it. The creature seems to have vanished."

He sighed heavily. "I suppose you're right. It would be nice if I had someone to talk it over with, though."

"What am I, chopped liver?"

"Sorry. You know what I mean. You have Wilma and I usually talk about guy things with Bob. But I've sworn you to secrecy and sworn myself to secrecy. I haven't said a word to no one."

"Neither have I," Marg said, her eyes misting up. "This is something we'll have to deal with together. Just the two of us."

Thor pushed his half-eaten meal away and Marg noticed for the first time that now even his normally gargantuan appetite was being affected by the mysterious beast.

"It makes me feel rather stupid," Thor said. "I should've believed all your other ghost stories and stuff. Then I wouldn't be so fucked up by this one."

I hate to say I told you so. "Well, I don't wanna turn your beliefs upside down. But I think it'll eventually make it easier if you just accept it and try and move on. You can dismiss it out of hand, but, really, can you live a lie and try and convince yourself over time that what your eyes saw and your ears heard never really happened?"

"You know what they say..." Thor said.

"Remind me."

"If you repeat something long enough it becomes true to you."

Marg spread her arms, hands raised, palms up. "Up to you, ultimately, how you want to deal with it. But I'm not sure it's healthy to have both of us on opposite sides of the fence on something we both witnessed."

Thor frowned, looking forlornly at his plate. "I guess you're right. I'll just have to get over it. And I'll have to get over the guilt." His tone grew more emotional. "Do you know how many times I've told people they're full of shit when they started talking about some supernatural shit... err... stuff? How many times have I told you to stop talking nonsense when you've brought up ghosts or demons?"

"I don't care about that now. I'm worried about your mental health. About our relationship. You never believed before because you never had proof. There are millions, if not billions, of people in the world like you were. But now you have proof. Now you can't categorically deny the existence of such things."

After a long and thoughtful pause, Thor's face brightened. Marg could almost see the heavy cloud of stress beginning to float away.

"Okay, I'll agree to try to believe. If you'll agree to something."

"Anything."

"Anything?" Thor asked, a twinkle in his eye.

She shifted in her chair, catching the sexual innuendo. "Anything in the bedroom and anything within reason outside of the bedroom."

He grinned, a first in three days. "I'm referring to outside of the bedroom but I might not be averse to something in the bedroom."

"Just say what you mean."

"I just don't wanna talk about it anymore," Thor said. "As long as it doesn't return, we won't discuss it. Can you agree to that?"

"Sure. We've hardly mentioned it in the last three days."

Thor pushed his chair back quickly and stood. He bent over and kissed Marg full on the lips, a first in about two months. "We've got a deal. And I have a little surprise for you tonight."

"You do?"

"Yes, I'll show it to you. In the bedroom. Later."

To celebrate their new understanding, Marg drained an entire bottle of wine and Thor pounded back at least half a bottle of whiskey. Later that evening, he was like a tiger in bed and Marg moaned and writhed in exquisite pleasure as his hands and tongue found and freely explored all of her erogenous zones. She reciprocated ravenously, pleasuring her husband more intensely than she had in many months.

When they'd finished, she lay in bed, mentally and physically satisfied, studying a thin line of moonlight poking through the half-opened blinds. It moved across the ceiling, probably guided by wind-blown passing clouds. She sighed deeply and smiled. *Maybe this monster thing is a blessing in disguise.*

***

It was meant to be a pre-Christmas party. Thor's boss, Bob Krieger, and his wife, Filomena, and Marg's best friend, Wilma Phipps, and her husband, Gary, would soon be arriving at the Davenport residence for a dinner party. It was December 1st. Since both couples had other more family-connected plans for Christmas, they'd decided a pre-Christmas party would afford the best chance of seeing each other before the busy holiday season kicked into high gear.

Thor entered the kitchen, clean-cut and clean-shaven, just as Marg removed the beef lasagna from the oven. He hugged her from behind and one hand brushed across the nipple of one pendulous breast. It sent a warm and tingling sensation through her body.

"Looks delicious," he said, kissing her on the cheek and gliding his tongue toward her earlobe.

"Not now," she mock-scolded. "We have plenty of time for that."

"As long as we kick them out early enough," Thor said with a wink.

Marg set the lasagna on a hot plate and began tossing a salad. "I didn't make turkey. Do you think they'll mind?"

"No, honey. They'll be eating so much turkey over Christmas they'll probably turn into one."

She pecked him on the cheek. "You're right, as always."

"Not always," he said. "Only sometimes. I hear a car. Oh, that's Bob's truck."

She waved him away. "Go welcome the guests and leave me in the kitchen. You're just a hindrance here."

"Maybe in the kitchen," he said with a grin. "But not in the bedroom."

"Oh, stop it," she said, a giant smile brightening her face.

As Thor welcomed the guests, Marg thought about what he'd said. Not necessarily the part about Thor being far from a hindrance in the bedroom (although that thought tantalizingly tickled her thoughts), but more about him admitting that he wasn't always right. Since their discussion some months ago, Thor had been true to his word, choosing to believe in but forget about the monster. And they'd both kept their promises. While the monster had on occasion entered Marg's thoughts, and probably Thor's, they hadn't mentioned a word of it to one another. It was as if they'd literally willed it away. And since their agreement, they hadn't seen a sign of it. They were loath to admit they were both too scared to revisit the site that once had, and probably still did, contain all of the evidence. *There will be time for that*, Marg thought. As long as the evidence was buried under a thick blanket of snow, it was out of sight and out of mind. Good enough. For now.

After an enjoyable dinner, some light-hearted conversation, and a few drinks, the guests and the hosts retired to the living room.

Bob, a bearded man with shortly cropped gray hair, sat next to his wife, a tiny woman with long and flowing black hair that she continuously stroked, perhaps recognizing it as one of her most striking attributes.

Wilma and Gary, both pleasingly plump and often smiling, took the opposite couch and sat hand in hand.

Thor and Marg both settled for armchairs, facing their guests.

"I sure hope this weather gives us a break," Marg said, starting the conversation off with something all Canadians were obsessed with talking about. "I hope all this snow doesn't mean winter is here to stay."

"It *is* December after all," Bob said, putting a hand on Filomena's knee. She twirled a lock of her hair and nodded to her husband.

"Have you seen all the animal tracks out there now?" Bob asked.

That was still a touchy subject for Marg. She nodded.

"I haven't noticed any more than usual for this time of the year," Thor said, pulling on his glass of whiskey, his eyes widening barely perceptibly

"Well, your neighbor up the road sure has," Wilma said.

"What neighbor?" Marg asked.

"Stan, that guy a half mile up the road," Wilma said.

"I don't think we should get into that," Gary said, releasing his wife's hand. "Everyone knows he's nuts."

Every small community has one. Or more. Stan Sizemore was known around the area as "out there," to say the least. He lived off the grid, mostly kept to himself, and presented himself as a wild animal in public. He was ill-mannered, grumpy, and wanted very little to do with people. A misanthrope, to be sure. His property was a mess of vehicles and other junk that he supposedly recycled for his livelihood. Marg and Thor had nothing to do with him, and Stan would've been perfectly happy with that arrangement. He was also known as a big drinker, and on a few occasions had been spotted by locals staggering around his junk pile of a property, slamming into obstacles and falling down at random. Rumor had it he'd lived a loveless childhood. Still, other rumors purported that his loving family lived in New Brunswick and it had been Stan who'd unceremoniously cut off ties for no apparent reason. People just believed what they wanted to believe but few people had anything to do with him, preferring instead to leave him wallowing in the comfort or discomfort of his solitary existence, as was his want.

Marg crossed her legs and sipped wine. "I don't wanna talk about him."

But Thor pressed on. "What'd he say?"

"You mean you haven't heard?" Wilma said. "I thought local gossip travels faster than the fastest internet."

"I think we should leave this alone," Gary said.

"If it's a rumor, you guys are bound to find out anyway," Bob said. "You may as well tell them."

To Bob, Thor said, "Have you heard the story?"

"No," Bob said.

Thor looked at his wife pleadingly. "We're gonna find out anyway, hon. We'll be curious and wanna know. You know how that goes."

Marg put down her wine glass. Darkness began to sweep over her otherwise merry mood and she didn't like where this was going. But she knew her husband was right. All it would take was one little supply run into town for her to get an earful of different versions of the rumor about Stan.

To Wilma, Marg said, "Okay, what's the latest gossip?"

Wilma rubbed her hands together, relishing the telling. "Stan went into the Esso in Millar River the other day. He was totally hysterical. He said he saw a large monster on his property, footprints about two feet long, and large claw marks on a tree that he claimed the monster had demolished."

Marg felt the color draining from her face as a chill crept over her, in spite of the roaring fire.

Thor spilled some of his drink, wiping drops of whiskey from his chin, and setting his glass down with an unsteady hand.

The words were slow to come, but Marg forced them. "How does this story end?"

"Apparently, he pleaded with people to come and see the footprints and the damage, but everyone chalked it up to his insanity and refused to bother. I guess what's strange about it is, normally, Stan is anti-social and reclusive. For him to behave like that, it almost makes one think something *did* happen."

Gary turned to his wife. "But you don't believe it?"

"No. Not when you consider the source."

"I don't believe it, that's for sure," Gary said.

"I don't believe in stuff like that," Filomena said.

"I don't believe it either," Bob said. "I'd need proof. It's probably just booze and drug-fueled hallucinations. I hear he's a big pot smoker. Who knows what other chemicals he abuses."

Looking at Thor and then at Marg, Wilma said, "What about you guys?"

Marg and Thor looked at each other, both wearing masks of confusion and doubt.

"You don't believe that bullshit?" Bob asked Thor. "Do you?"

"I'm sorry," Thor said, "but I'm not gonna weigh in on it."

"No comment, huh?" Bob said. "What about you, Marg?"

"I believe in the supernatural, so I'm not ruling anything out."

"You gotta be kidding me?" Bob said, snickering.

Even Filomena was unable to conceal a small laugh.

"Well, each to their own," Marg said, feeling the veins in her neck pulsating with a fresh surge of blood.

"You guys look like you've seen a ghost," Gary said. "I think we should drop this."

"Did you guys see monster tracks?" Bob said, unwilling to drop it.

Filomena giggled and Bob squeezed her hand, stemming the rising tide of laughter.

There was a feeling, not entirely unfamiliar to Marg, that to lie about the monster's existence would be to disrespect it. She was unwilling to wade onto thin ice. She was also cognizant of the miraculous transformation in her husband, a metamorphosis that evidently had only come to fruition as a result of his willingness to admit that he believed the monster existed. What would it mean to deny its existence? Yet, did she want to make a fool out of herself in front of her guests?

She was stuck between a rock and hard place. She didn't know what to do.

Fortunately, Thor made the decision for her. "Okay, I *will* weigh in on it. I never used to believe in the supernatural, or monsters, or ghosts, or demons, but now I do."

"I believe as well," Marg said, deciding to stand by her man.

"Let me continue, honey."

"You have the floor, my dear."

"Good," he said. "Like you, Bob, I was the eternal doubter. I dismissed it all as creative fiction. That was up until a few months ago when I saw something. Saw proof. It scared the hell out of me. But it also taught me something. Don't disbelieve in something you know nothing about. To do so becomes hypocrisy, or ignorance. And otherworldly creatures don't take too kindly to ignorance in us humans. They might one day decide to tear you a new asshole. Quite literally."

A hush fell over the room and a few mouths dropped to the floor. Filomena stifled a snicker, covering her mouth with both hands.

Wilma and Gary's eyes widened, some color draining from their faces, and said nothing.

However, Bob, perhaps fueled by liquor, wanted clarification. "What did you see?" he demanded with a mocking grin and an equally mocking tone.

Filomena was unable to stifle a snicker.

"We saw—"

Thor leaped to his feet, a large vein snaking and pulsating across his forehead. "No, Marg, don't."

"Why not?" Bob said. "It seems to me like a great night for spooky stories by the fire."

"No," Thor insisted. "You're not ready. None of you are ready."

"I'll tell you what I'm ready for," Wilma said, standing, yawning, and pulling Gary to his feet. "I'm ready for bed."

Bob took the cue, pulling his wife to her feet. "I think it's time to go."

***

After everyone had left, albeit rather unceremoniously, Marg busied herself in the kitchen cleaning up. For a rare change, Thor helped her, putting all the dishes on the countertop. Thor put the leftovers away while Marg scrubbed pots and pans.

They went about the cleanup silently, and when Thor finished, he headed toward the living room.

"Would you like tea or hot chocolate?" Marg asked as he stepped into the hallway.

He turned around. "Hot chocolate, please. I'm done with the whiskey."

"Hot chocolate it is. I'll join you in a minute."

"Okay."

"And Thor?"

"Yeah."

"I'm proud of you."

He looked defeated. "I'm not too proud of myself. Should've kept my big mouth shut."

A few minutes later, Marg joined Thor in the living room. They sat huddled around the wood stove, Marg sipping herbal tea and Thor drinking hot chocolate.

After a few minutes of wordless reflection, Marg broke the silence. "I think you *had* to say what you said. It's unwise to disrespect or disbelieve in entities we know nothing about. You were right."

The lines snaking across Thor's brow suggested he was far from convinced. "I don't really care if Gary or Wilma believe us or not. Or even Filomena, that little mocking bitch. But Bob's my boss. What if he fires me over this?"

"He won't fire you. You've been a loyal and hard-working employee for a long time. What would he do without you? Your beliefs have nothing to do with your job performance. He should respect that."

"Everyone is replaceable, hon. Once you start thinking you're not, that's usually when you get replaced."

Marg had to admit her husband had a point. And they needed the job, needed the income. What was the solution? So convinced was she that to deny the existence of the monster would lead to disastrous consequences, she knew it was too late for Thor to do an about-face and claim he'd been joking about his new-found belief in monsters. Besides, his manner and tone when he'd confessed his convictions earlier were far from flippant. No, that wouldn't work. What then?

"I'm gonna call Bob and apologize," Thor said. "Maybe I'll just tell him we should agree to disagree."

They spent the next ten minutes carefully crafting the words Thor planned on saying to his boss. They went like this: *Bob, I want to apologize for my self-righteous tone tonight. Maybe I should've kept my mouth shut, or at least toned it down. I understand that you don't believe in the supernatural or anything like that, and I should've respected your opinion. I hope that you can respect my opinion and we can agree to disagree. I hope this won't become an obstacle to our business relationship or friendship. I hope you can find it in your heart to forgive me. Maybe some things are better left unsaid and maybe this is one of them. Can we please put it behind us and not discuss it anymore?*

But the phone call went to voicemail, and Thor hung up without leaving a message. He looked downtrodden and sad. "Shit. I wonder if he's mad at me."

Marg wanted to put a stop to it before the seeds of doubt festered into weeds of paranoia that could potentially keep Thor up all night, fretting and fuming. "Don't worry about it, dear. Call him first thing—"

A loud growl rattled the house and its inhabitants.

Thor rushed to the window and pointed. "Look!"

Marg was right behind him. She saw it too. In the driveway, visible in the full moon and gently falling snow, was a gigantic black being, its furry head enormous in comparison to its massive body.

In the dark of the night, its beady red eyes glowed ominously.

"Oh my God," Marg said.

Thor was already running for the door, and before Marg could even register her fear, he was throwing on his boots and jacket and slipping a flashlight into his pocket.

"You... you can't go out," Marg said.

"I... I have to... I have to make sure everything's okay."

Marg quickly went to the closet and pulled out her winter jacket. "Then I'm coming with you."

"No, you're not."

"Yes I am," she said, putting on her boots. "I couldn't live with myself if something happened to you and I could've done something about it and didn't. This is not open for negotiation."

Thor reached into the closet and retrieved another flashlight. "Then take this."

Outside, they walked the length of their 200-foot driveway without seeing a single track. No trace of the monster. But when they reached the snow-covered two-lane highway, Thor stopped and pointed down the road.

"You see that?" he said.

Marg squinted but couldn't see anything. Then she did see it—a flashing red light about three-quarters of a mile away. "Oh, no."

"Come on," Thor said, leading Marg to his vehicle. "Let's go check it out."

***

As they arrived at the scene, a flashlight-wielding cop waved them over to the shoulder. A police cruiser blocked the road. Behind it, two ambulances were parked. A man on a stretcher was being loaded into an ambulance by two paramedics. Two other paramedics were securing the rear doors to the second ambulance.

Pulling onto the shoulder, Thor shuddered. He recognized the wreckage of Bob's pickup. It was wrapped around a power pole, and the pole was teetering at a dangerous angle.

Marg gasped at the sight. "Oh my God… please, God, no."

As a cop approached Thor's pickup, Marg saw sparks shooting from wires at the top of the power pole, zapping, popping, and sizzling.

The cop tapped the driver's-side window with his flashlight and Thor rolled it down. "You can't stay here," he said. "I'm sorry but you're gonna have to turn around. As you can see, we're investigating an accident scene and that live power pole could come down at any second and kill you."

"They're our friends, Bob and Filomena," Thor said. "They were just at our place for dinner. Are they gonna be okay?"

"I don't know," the cop said. "They were both smashed up pretty badly. I'm no doctor, but I'm told both of them are unconscious."

The cop quickly took their names, phone number, and address, and told them he would call them later with some questions and an update. "But, right now, you gotta get outta here."

Thor turned the pickup around and left.

Marg gripped the dashboard safety handle with both hands, her knuckles whitening as the severity of what they'd just witnessed began to settle in.

"Drive by Wilma's," she said. "Just to make sure their car's in the driveway."

They proceeded silently down the highway, and eventually, Thor stopped in front of Wilma and Gary's driveway, which was only a few thousand feet from Thor and Marg's house.

Seeing Wilma's porchlight on and the gleam of her SUV from the light's reflection, Thor and Marg simultaneously breathed a sigh of relief.

"Thank God," Thor said.

Suddenly, Thor's truck headlights illuminated something. Something dark and sinister.

"Oh, no... PLEASE, GOD, NO!" Marg shrieked.

Large footprints—about two feet long and ten feet apart—led to Wilma and Gary's driveway, stopping abruptly at their open front door.

Misanthrope

On a winter afternoon, Guy Hendrickson sat on a log on the sandy shore of Poverty Beach in Prince Edward Island ruminating about his miserable state of being.

The sunny sky, puffy clouds, deep blue waters, and gently splashing waves did nothing to brighten his sour mood.

He knew he wasn't a very sociable person. He always told people, "The more people I meet, the more I like my cat." Except he didn't own a cat.

He also knew he wasn't that likable. People always told him, "You're about as likable as cat shit in your bed." Except he didn't have cat shit in his bed. Not without a cat.

Guy had once owned a black-and-white cat. But he'd yelled at Felix one too many times and Felix had disappeared. Two weeks later, he saw Felix perched contentedly on a neighbor's porch a few blocks away. He was tempted to walk straight past the home without acknowledging Felix, but some strange and mysterious feeling of compassion had swept over him and he'd stopped.

"Felix," he'd said.

Felix arched his back, puffed his tail, hissed, and disappeared.

So now, who did Guy have in his life? His parents were long-dead, fatalities in a plane crash. His two brothers and three sisters had disowned him decades ago. Or he'd disowned them. Whatever. His five friends had disappeared from his life like scared rabbits. Or scared cats.

"You're about as likable as cat shit in your bed."

Of course, there was her, he thought, gazing out at but not seeing the brilliant blue sky and magnificent view out to sea. Although he still couldn't bring himself to say her name, she was the only person in his miserable life who'd actually meant something to him. Guy was 67, two years into his Canada Pension Plan now. She had come into his life two decades ago, the only girlfriend he'd ever had, the only woman he'd ever loved.

It had lasted three years before his foul temper, wretched disposition, and outright unwarranted hostility toward her had resulted in her fiery exodus. She'd erupted into a rage one afternoon after he'd picked a fight with her over nothing.

After hurling a litany of profanity at him, she'd parted company with one last shot: "You're about as likable as cat shit in your bed."

But, he remembered now, she'd added something. Something he'd blocked for so many years: "So go fuck yourself!!!"

He looked around, disbelieving for a second that he'd said it aloud. There was no one around. Poverty Beach, perhaps living up to its namesake, was abandoned.

"Who the fuck are you?" Guy said. "Who the fuck am I?"

"You're a misanthrope," a voice from behind him said. "That's what you are."

Guy spun around.

An old man with a cane stood about ten feet away. He was hunchbacked, his skin as cracked and creviced as a dehydrated desert river bed. Large black circles framed his gray eyes.

Where did he come from? "What did you say?"

"You're a misanthrope," the man said.

"What the hell is a misanthrope?"

"A person who hates humankind and avoids human society."

"So go fuck yourself!" Guy said.

He turned and faced the ocean, but then spun around and was about to add another profanity-laced rebuke when he realized the man was gone. He'd disappeared as quickly as he'd appeared.

But Guy was way beyond questioning it or even viewing it as some kind of an epiphany. He stood up, stripped naked, and waded out into the water.

An incoming wave crashed over his ankles and he shivered. It was cold. Freezing fucking cold. As he walked out into deep waters, he wondered what would kill him first—death by drowning or death by hypothermia.

"Probably drowning," he said, now waist-deep in the frigid ocean water. When the water was too deep to walk, he began treading water, shaking like a wind-blown snowflake in a ferocious blizzard.

He dunked his head under, held his breath for a few seconds, resurfaced, and swallowed a mouthful of salt water. He coughed several times and started moving his extremities rapidly in an ill-fated effort to keep warm.

Then something—no someone—caught his eye. He focused his aging eyes on the shoreline. A woman with frilly brown hair stood on the water's edge. She wore a long black trench coat and matching black boots. She was waving at him.

Guy couldn't believe his eyes. He said her name for the first time in twenty years. "Cassandra!"

A large grin spread across her face.

"So go fuck yourself," she said.

A large wave precipitously appeared, crashed over Guy, and washed him out to sea. His lungs filled with water and he bubbled up the last vestiges of life.

Guy woke up drenched in sweat, heart pounding, puking and coughing, the nightmare was that powerful and real. He fell out of bed, landed on all fours, and continued puking for a full minute. When he finally regained a semblance of composure, he stood shakily and began staggering toward his bedroom door. *If you ever had a second chance, this is it.*

The phone on his bedside table rang for the first time in twenty years. Even bill collectors and phone solicitors had better things to do. The ringing sound almost gave him a heart attack.

He wobbled over and picked up the dust-laden handset.

"Hell... hello?"

"Guy?"

He almost fainted right then and there.

"Cass... Cassandra?"

"Yes, it's me. I just called to check in on you."

"You're not gonna tell me to go fuck myself, are you?"

"Not right now. Maybe after I get to know you again."

The End

Also By William Blackwell

Phantom Rage, Poison Rage, Infected Rage
Nightmare's Edge
Resurrection Point
Brainstorm
A Head for an Eye
Rule 14
Assaulted Souls
Assaulted Souls II
Assaulted Souls III
Blood Curse
Black Dawn
The Strap
The End is Nigh
Orgon Conclusion
Freaky Franky
The Witch's Tombstone
The Dark Menace
In Your Dreams
Tales of Damnation
Lunatics

In Your Dreams Preview

Alienated from humanity, Oliver Gimble is a self-indulgent sloth who finds vicarious comfort in binge-watching horror movies and gorging on junk food. During sleep, he escapes into a meticulously constructed dream world where he discovers carnal delight with an enigmatic woman called Stella.

His bizarre lifestyle begins to unravel when he meets Carmen Weathersby, a lonely woman, who in Oliver's mind's eye mysteriously transforms into Stella, the woman of his dreams. But soon Oliver realizes Stella is actually interfering with his new relationship and will go to any lengths, even murder, to possess him.

When Carmen's elderly mother suffers a heart attack, fingers point at Stella.

Suddenly, people close to Carmen start dying—brutally and inexplicably.

Careening helplessly down into a cryptic and otherworldly realm somewhere between reality and perception, Carmen and Oliver desperately try to solve the macabre mystery before it's too late.

A multi-layered, horrifying journey of self-discovery, *In Your Dreams* examines the powerful and shocking connections between our conscious and subconscious worlds—boldly questioning the very nature of reality.

"On the surface, it's a gripping horror thriller with brutal, shocking twists. But beneath that, it's a thought-provoking exploration of obsession, loneliness, and the terrifying power our subconscious holds over us. The writing is bold, cinematic, and immersive—it reminded me of a cross between Clive Barker and early Stephen King, yet with a unique, modern edge." Amazon

About the Author

Canadian dark fiction author William Blackwell studied journalism at Mount Royal University and English literature at The University of British Columbia. He worked as a journalist and a newspaper editor for many years before pursuing his passion for storytelling. His novels have been characterized as graphic, edgy, and at times terrifying. Currently living on a secluded acreage on Prince Edward Island, Blackwell finds much of his inspiration from Mother Nature, odd people, traveling, and bizarre nightmares.

Author Comments

Thank you for reading this book. I would be eternally grateful if you would post a book review on your favorite book retailer's website. A positive review is the highest compliment a writer can receive. Reviews are crucial to the success of any author. You don't have to say much. A few sentences will suffice.

In other news, I have a gift for you. Complete the signup form below with your name and email address and download a FREE copy of *Resurrection Point*, a dark tale about the horrifying consequences of experimenting with death and resurrection. You're only agreeing to be kept up to date on blog posts, new releases, and freebies. I promise I won't spam you and you can unsubscribe at any time.

Thanks again for your support.

http://www.wblackwell.com/free-ebook/